Martha LeBaron Goddard, Harriet Waters Preston

Sea and Shore

A Collection of Poems

Martha LeBaron Goddard, Harriet Waters Preston

Sea and Shore
A Collection of Poems

ISBN/EAN: 9783742812360

Manufactured in Europe, USA, Canada, Australia, Japa

Cover: Foto ©Andreas Hilbeck / pixelio.de

Manufactured and distributed by brebook publishing software
(www.brebook.com)

Martha LeBaron Goddard, Harriet Waters Preston

Sea and Shore

AND SHORE.

A Collection of Poems.

"The current sweeps the old world,
  The current sweeps the new;
  The wind will blow, the dawn will glow,
  Ere thou hast sailed them through."

CHARLES KINGSLEY.

BOSTON:

ROBERTS BROTHERS.

1874.

-

Cambridge:
Press of John Wilson and Son.

*A*ND ever, as he travelled, he would climb
     The farthest mountain; yet the heavenly chime,
The mighty tolling of the far-off spheres
Beating their pathway, never touched his ears.
But wheresoe'er he rose the heavens rose,
And the far-gazing mountain could disclose
Nought but a wider earth; until one height
Showed him the ocean stretched in liquid light,
And he could hear its multitudinous roar,
Its plunge and hiss upon the pebbled shore.
Then Jubal silent sat, and touched his lyre no more.

He thought, " This world is great : but I am weak,
And where the sky bends is no solid peak
To give me footing; but, instead, this main,
Like myriad maddened horses thundering o'er the
     plain."

GEORGE ELIOT

SEA AND SHORE.

THE DESCENT OF NEPTUNE.

From the Iliad of Homer, Book XIII.

NO careless watch the monarch Neptune kept:
    Wond'ring he viewed the battle where he sat
Aloft on wooded Samos' topmost peak,
Samos, of Thrace; whence Ida's heights he saw,
And Priam's city, and the ships of Greece.
Thither ascended from the sea, he sat;
And thence the Greeks by Trojans overborne
Pitying he saw, and deeply wroth with Jove.
Then down the mountain's craggy side he passed
With rapid step; and, as he moved along,
Beneath the immortal feet of Ocean's Lord
Quaked the huge mountain and the shadowy wood.
Three strides he took; the fourth he reached his goal,
Aigæ, where on the margin of the bay
His temple stood, all glittering, all of gold
Imperishable; there arrived, he yoked
Beneath his car the brazen-footed steeds,
Of swiftest flight, with manes of flowing gold.
All clad in gold, the golden lash he grasped,
Of curious work, and, mounting on his car,
Skimmed o'er the waves; from all the depths below

Gambolled around the monsters of the deep,
Acknowledging their king ; the joyous sea
Parted her waves ; swift flew the bounding steeds ;
Nor was the brazen axle wet with spray,
When to the ships of Greece their Lord they bore.
Down in the deep recesses of the sea
A spacious cave there is, which lies midway
'Twixt Tenedos and Imbros' rocky isle ;
Earth-shaking Neptune there his coursers stayed,
Loosed from the chariot, and before them placed
Ambrosial provender ; and round their feet
Shackles of gold, which none might break or loose,
That there they might await their Lord's return ;
Then to the Grecian army took his way.

LORD DERBY

THE DESCENT OF NEPTUNE.

From the Iliad of Homer, Book XIII.

THE monarch Neptune kept no idle watch ;
   For he in Thracian Samos, dark with woods,
Aloft upon the highest summit sat,
O'erlooking thence the tumult of the war ;
For thence could he behold the Idæan mount,
And Priam's city, and the Grecian fleet.
There, coming from the ocean deeps, he sat,
And pitied the Greek warriors put to rout
Before the Trojans, and was wroth with Jove.
Soon he descended from those rugged steeps,

And trod the earth with rapid strides ; the hills
And forests quaked beneath the immortal feet
Of Neptune as he walked.   Three strides he took,
And at the fourth reached Aegæ, where he stopped,
And where his sumptuous palace halls were built,
Deep down in ocean, golden, glittering, proof
Against decay of time.   These when he reached,
He yoked his swift and brazen-footed steeds,
With manes of flowing gold, to draw his car,
And put on golden mail and took his scourge
Wrought of fine gold, and climbed the chariot seat
And rode upon the waves.   The whales came forth
From their deep haunts, and frolicked round his way.
They knew their king.   The waves rejoicing smoothed
A path, and rapidly the coursers flew ;
Nor was the brazen axle wet below,
And thus they brought him to the Grecian fleet.

WILLIAM CULLEN BRYANT.

VISIT OF THE ARGONAUTS TO THE CAVE OF CHIRON.

From Onomacritus.

THEN with a whistling breeze did Juno fill the
    sail,
And Argo self-impelled shot swift before the gale.
The kings with nerve and heart the oar unwearied
    plied ;
Ploughed by the keel, foamed white the immeasurable
    tide.

But when from Ocean's streams the sacred dawn
    appeared,
And morning's pleasant light both gods and mortals
    cheered ;
Then, from the shore, the rocks and windy summits
    high
Of wood-topt Pelion reared their beacon midst the sky.
The helm, with both his hands, the pilot Tiphys held ;
The vessel cut the wave, with quiet course impelled ;
Then swift they neared the shore, the wooden ladder
    cast,
And forth the heroes leaped, relieved from labors past.

Sir C. A. Elton.

THE SAILING OF THE ARGO.

From Pindar.

AND soon as by the vessel's bow
    The anchor was hung up ;
Then took the leader on the prow,
    In hands, a golden cup ;
And on great father Jove did call ;
And on the winds, and waters all
Swept by the hurrying blast ;
And on the nights and ocean ways ;
And on the fair auspicious days,
And sweet return at last.
From out the clouds, in answer kind,
A voice of thunder came ;
And shook in glistering beams around,

Burst out the lightning flame.
The chiefs breathed free. and at the sign
Trusted in the power divine.
Hinting sweet hopes, the seer cried,
Forthwith their oars to ply ;
And swift went backward from rough hands
The rowing ceaselessly.

H. F. CARY.

ON THE TOMB OF A SHIPWRECKED MARINER.

From Posidippus.

A H, why, my brother mariner, so near the boister-
ous wave
Of ocean have ye hollowed out my solitary grave ?
'Twere better much that far from hence a sailor's tomb
should be,
For I dread my rude destroyer, I dread the roaring sea.
But may the smiles of fortune, may love and peace
await
All ye that shed a tear for poor Nicetas' hapless fate !

THE CALM OF EVENINC.

From Ennius.

T HE heaven's vast world stood silent ; Neptune
gave
A hushful pause to ocean's roughening wave ;
The sun curbed his swift steeds ; the eternal floods
Stood still ; and not a breath was on the woods.

WILLIAM PETER.

DANAË.

From Simonides. In the metre of the original.

BY the billows and blast driven and tost in the gloom
    Of the tempest-night, cowering in terror
Sat she, and clasped to her arms little Perseus,
And wept sore, many a moan uttering,
In anguish of heart: O my darling child,
Misery crushes me ; but in soft slumber reposing
Carest thou not, fearest thou nought, innocent one !
Here, in the cold, rayless, desolate gloom,
Warm is thy rest, fair is thy couch, royal its hue —
    beautiful face !
Couldst thou but know what is thy dreadful doom,
Hadst thou an ear ready to listen
To these my words — Nay, thou shalt sleep, — baby
    shall sleep !
Fall asleep, thou mighty ocean ! sleep, O my misery !
In vain they weave their wicked plans, O Father !
Wilt thou not — Zeus, I beseech ! — destroy all they
    have willed ?
For the child I pray ; fearless, I claim — vengeance !

D. F. L.

DANAË.

From Simonides.

THERE was once a carven ark adrift on a stormy
    sea ;
And the wind in each crevice shrieked, and Danaë
    cowering there,

With the spray on her cheeks and screening her Per-
seus motherly,
Crooned him a song like this in the midst of her de-
spair :
" O baby, mother is full of heavy care ; but thou
Hast sucked thyself asleep and liest without a dream,
In the dismal brass-bound house, where on thy quiet
brow
Strikes through the murky gloom the night-lamp's fitful
gleam.
And the wind pipes loud and shrill, and the wave goes
o'er thy head ;
But thou dost not heed it, sweet, — thy clustering curls
are dry,
Beautiful little face all swathed in its mantle red !
Ah, if thou didst but know my harrowing misery !
Heardest a tithe of my complaints ! — hush, dear ;
And hush, thou noisy sea ! and sleep, my sorrow wild !
And baffle their counsel, father Zeus, who left us here !
Nay, I am bold to say, be just to the blameless child ! "

H. W. P.

WOULD GOD I WERE NOW BY THE SEA !

From Euripides.

WOULD God I were now by the sea !
By the winding wet-worn caves,
By the ragged rents of the rocks !
And that there as a bird I might be
White-winged with the sea-skimming flocks ;

Where the spray and the breeze blow free
 O'er the ceaseless mirth of the waves,
 And dishevel their loose gray locks.
I would spread my wings to the moist, salt air,
And my wide white wings should carry me
 Lifted up out over the sea, —
 Carry I heed not where,
 Somewhither far away,
Somewhither far from my hateful home,
Where the breast of the breeze is sprinkled with spray,
Where the restless deep is maddened with glee ;
 Over the waves' wild ecstasy,
 Through the wild blown foam !

W. H. M.

THE CONTRAST.

From Moschus.

O'ER the smooth main, when scarce a zephyr blows
 To break the dark blue ocean's deep repose,
I seek the calmness of the breathing shore,
Delighted with the fields and woods no more.

But when white-foaming heave the deeps on high,
Swells the black storm and mingles sea with sky,
Trembling I fly the wild tempestuous strand,
And seek the close recesses of the land.

Sweet are the sounds that murmur through the wood,
While roaring storms upheave the dangerous flood ;

Then if the winds more fiercely howl, they rouse
But sweeter music in the pines' tall boughs.

Hard is the life the weary fisher finds,
Who trusts his floating mansion to the winds,
Whose daily food the fickle sea maintains,
Unchanging labor and uncertain gains.

Be mine soft sleep, beneath the spreading shade
Of some broad leafy plane inglorious laid,
Lulled by a fountain's fall that, murmuring near,
Soothes, not alarms, the toil-worn laborer's ear.

ROBERT BLAND.

THE RETURN OF SPRING TO THE SAILOR.

From Philostratus.

HASTE to the port! The twittering swallow calls,
    Again returned; the wintry breezes sleep;
The meadows laugh; and warm the zephyr falls
    On ocean's breast, and calms the fearful deep.

Now spring your cables, loiterers! Spread your sails!
    O'er the smooth surface of the water roam!
So shall your vessel glide with friendly gales,
    And fraught with foreign treasure waft you home.

THE LOOSING OF THE WINDS.

From the Æneid of Virgil, Book I.

HE said, and with his spear struck wide
    The portals of the mountain side.
At once, like soldiers in a band,
Forth rush the winds, and scour the land;
Then lighting heavily on the main,
East, South, and West, with storms in train,
Heave from its depth the watery floor,
And roll great billows to the shore.
Then come the clamour and the shriek,
The sailors shout, the main-ropes creak:
All in a moment sun and skies
Are blotted from the Trojans' eyes;
Black night is brooding o'er the deep,
Sharp thunder peals, live lightnings leap;
The stoutest warrior holds his breath,
And looks as on the face of death.
At once Æneas thrilled with dread:
Forth from his breast, with hands outspread,
These groaning words he drew:
"O happy thrice and yet again,
Who died at Troy like valiant men,
    E'en in their parents' view!
O Diomed, first of Greeks in fray,
Why pressed I not the plain that day,
    Yielding my life to you,

Where stretched beneath a Phrygian sky
Fierce Hector, tall Sarpedon, lie ;
Where Simoïs tumbles 'neath his wave
Shields, helms, and bodies of the brave ? "

Now, howling from the North, the gale,
While thus he moans him, strikes his sail ;
The swelling surges climb the sky ;
The shattered oars in splinters fly ;
The prow turns round, and to the tide
Lays broad and bare the vessel's side ;
On comes a billow, mountain-steep,
Bears down, and tumbles in a heap.
These stagger on the billows' crest ;
Those to the yawning depth deprest
See land appearing 'mid the waves,
While surf with sand in turmoil raves.
Three ships the South has caught and thrown
On scarce-hid rocks, as Altars known,
Ridging the main, a reef of stone.
Three more fierce Eurus from the deep,
A sight to make the gazer weep,
Drives on the shoals, and banks them round
With sand, as with a rampire-mound.
One, which erewhile from Lycia's shore
Orontes and his people bore,
E'en in Æneas' anguished sight,
A sea down crashing from the height
Strikes full astern ; the pilot, torn
From off the helm, is headlong borne ;
Three turns the foundered vessel gave,
Then sank beneath the engulfing wave.

There in the vast abyss are seen
The swimmers, few and far between ;
And warriors' arms and shattered wood
And Trojan treasures strew the flood.
And now Ilioneus, and now
    Aletes old and gray,
Abas and brave Achates bow
    Beneath the tempest's sway ;
Fast drinking in through timbers loose
At every pore the fatal ooze,
    Their sturdy barks give way.

JOHN CONINGTON.

THE LOOSING OF THE WINDS.

From the Æneid of Virgil, Book I.

THUS having said, with his inverted spear
    He smote the hollow mountain on the side.
Then forth the winds, like some great marching host,
Vent being given, rush turbulent, and blow
In whirling storm abroad upon the lands :
Down pressing on the sea from lowest depths
Upturned, Eurus and Notus all in one
Blowing, and Africus with rainy squalls,
Dense on the vast waves rolling to the shore.
Then follow clamoring shouts of men, and noise
Of whistling cordage. On a sudden, clouds
Snatch from the Trojans all the light of day
And the great sky. Black night lies on the sea.

The thunder rolls ; the incessant lightnings flash ;
And to the crews all bodes a present death.
Æneas' limbs relax with sudden cold ;
Groaning, his hands he stretches to the stars.
"Oh, thrice and four times happy they," he cries,
" To whom befell beneath Troy's lofty walls
To encounter death before their fathers' eyes !
O Diomed, thou bravest of the Greeks,
Why could I not have fallen on Ilium's fields,
Pouring my warm life out beneath thy hand ?
Where valiant Hector lies, by Achilles' spear
Slain, and where tall Sarpedon was o'erthrown,—
Where Simoïs rolls along, bearing away
Beneath his waves so many shields and casques,
So many corpses of brave heroes slain !"

Thus while he cried aloud, a roaring blast
From out the north strikes full against the sails,
And the waves touch the stars : the oars are snapped ;
The ship swings round, and gives to the waves its side.
A steep and watery mountain rolls apace :
Some on its summit hang ; and some beneath
Behold the earth between the yawning waves ;
Mingled with sand the boiling waters hiss.
On hidden rocks three ships the south wind hurls,
Rocks by the Italian sailors Altars called ;
A vast ridge on a level with the sea.
Three others by the East wind from the deep
Are driven upon the quicksands and the shoals, —
Dreadful to see, — upon the shallows dashed,
And girt around by drifting heaps of sand.

One, that conveyed the Lycians, and that bore
Faithful Orontes, there, before his eyes,
A huge sea from above strikes on the stern,
Dashing the pilot headlong on the waves.
Three times the surges whirl the ship around,
In the swift vortex of the sea engulfed ;
Then scattered swimmers in the vast abyss
Are seen, and arms and planks and Trojan spoils.
Now the strong ship of Ilioneus, now
Of brave Achates, and the barks that bore
Abas and old Aletes, are o'erwhelmed,
And all their yawning sides with loosened joints
Drink in the bitter drench.

CHRISTOPHER PEARSE CRANCH.

THE SONG OF THE ARGONAUTS.

From "The Life and Death of Jason."

O BITTER sea, tumultuous sea,
      Full many an ill is wrought by thee !
Unto the wasters of the land
Thou holdest out thy wrinkled hand ;
And when they leave the conquered town,
Whose black smoke makes thy surges brown,
Driven betwixt thee and the sun,
As the long day of blood is done,
From many a league of glittering waves
Thou smilest on them and their slaves.

The thin, bright-eyed Phenician
Thou drawest to thy waters wan ;
With ruddy eve and golden morn
Thou temptest him, until forlorn,
Unburied under alien skies
Cast up ashore his body lies.
Yea, whoso sees thee from his door
Must ever long for more and more ;
Nor will the beechen bowl suffice,
Or homespun robe of little price,
Or hood well-woven of the fleece
Undyed, or unspiced wine of Greece ;
So sore his heart is set upon
Purple and gold and cinnamon ;
For, as thou cravest, so he craves,
Until he rolls beneath thy waves.
Nor in some land-locked unknown bay
Can satiate thee for one day.

Now therefore, O thou bitter sea,
With no long words we pray to thee,
But ask thee, hast thou felt before
Such strokes of the long ashen oar ?
And hast thou yet seen such a prow
Thy rich and niggard waters plow ?
Nor yet, O sea, shalt thou be cursed,
If at thy hands we gain the worst,
And, wrapped in water, roll about
Blind-eyed, unheeding song or shout,
Within thine eddies far from shore,
Warmed by no sunlight any more.

Therefore indeed we joy in thee,
And praise thy greatness, and will we
Take at thy hands both good and ill,
Yea, what thou wilt, and praise thee still,
Enduring not to sit at home
And wait until the last days come,
When we no more may care to hold
White bosoms under crowns of gold,
And our dull hearts no longer are
Stirred by the clangorous noise of war,
And hope within our souls is dead
And no joy is rememberéd.

So, if thou hast a mind to slay,
Fair prize thou hast of us to-day;
And if thou hast a mind to save,
Great praise and honor shalt thou have:
But whatso thou wilt do with us,
Our end shall not be piteous,
Because our memories shall live
When folk forget the way to drive
The black keel through the heaped-up sea,
And half dried up thy waters be.

WILLIAM MORRIS.

THE SONG OF THE SIRENS.

From "The Life and Death of Jason."

ALAS! poor souls and timorous,
    Will ye draw nigh to gaze at us
And see if we are fair indeed,
For such as we shall be your meed,

There, where our hearts would have you go.
And where can the earth-dwellers show
In any land such loveliness
As that wherewith your eyes we bless,
O wanderers of the Minyæ,
Worn toilers over land and sea ?

If ye be bold with us to go,
Things such as happy dreams may show
Shall your once heavy eyes behold
About our palaces of gold ;
Where waters 'neath the waters run,
And from o'erhead a harmless sun
Gleams through the woods of chrysolite.
There gardens fairer to the sight
Than those of the Phæacian king
Shall ye behold ; and, wondering,
Gaze on the sea-born fruit and flowers,
And thornless and unchanging bowers,
Whereof the May-time knoweth nought.
So to the pillared house being brought,
Poor souls, ye shall not be alone ;
For o'er the floors of pale blue stone
All day such feet as ours shall pass,
And, 'twixt the glimmering walls of glass,
Such bodies garlanded with gold,
So faint, so fair, shall ye behold,
And clean forget the treachery
Of changing earth and tumbling sea.

Shall we not rise with you at night,
Up through the shimmering green twilight,

2

That maketh there our changeless day ;
Then going through the moonlight gray,
Shall we not sit upon those sands,
To think upon the troublous lands
Long left behind, where once ye were,
When every day brought change and fear ?
There, with white arms about you twined,
And shuddering somewhat at the wind
That ye rejoiced erewhile to meet,
Be happy, while old stories sweet,
Half-understood, float round your ears,
And fill your eyes with happy tears.

Ah ! while we sing unto you there,
As now we sing, with yellow hair
Blown round about these pearly limbs,
While underneath the gray sky swims
The light shell-sailor of the waves,
And, to our song, from sea-filled caves
Booms out an echoing harmony,
Shall ye not love the peaceful sea ?

Come to the land where none grows old
And none is rash or overbold,
Nor any noise there is, or war,
Or rumor from wild lands afar,
Or plagues, or birth and death of kings ;
No vain desire of unknown things
Shall vex you there, no hope or fear
Of that which never draweth near ;
But in that lovely land and still
Ye may remember what ye will,

And what ye will, forget for aye.
  So, while the kingdoms pass away,
Ye sea-beat, hardened toilers, erst
Unresting, for vain fame athirst,
Shall be at peace for evermore,
With hearts fulfilled with Godlike lore
And calm unwavering Godlike love,
No lapse of time can turn or move.
There, ages after your fair fleece
Is clean forgotten, yea, and Greece
Is no more counted glorious,
Alone with us, alone with us,
Alone with us dwell happily,
Beneath our trembling roof of sea.

WILLIAM MORRIS.

THE LOTOS-EATERS.

"COURAGE," he said, and pointed towards the
    land,
" This mounting wave will roll us shoreward soon."
In the afternoon they came unto a land
In which it seeméd always afternoon.
All round the coast the languid air did swoon,
Breathing like one that hath a weary dream.
Full-faced above the valley shone the moon ;
And, like a downward smoke, the slender stream
Along the cliff to fall, and pause and fall, did seem.

A land of streams ! Some, like a downward smoke,
Slow-dropping veils of thinnest lawn, did go ;

And some through wavering lights and shadows broke,
Rolling a slumberous sheet of foam below.
They saw the gleaming river seaward flow
From the inner land : far off, three mountain-tops,
Three silent pinnacles of aged snow,
Stood sunset-flushed ; and, dewed with showery drops,
Up-clomb the shadowy pine above the woven copse.

The charméd sunset lingered low adown
In the red West ; through mountain clefts the dale
Was seen far inland, and the yellow down
Bordered with palm, and many a winding vale
And meadow set with slender galingale ;
A land where all things always seemed the same !
And round about the keel with faces pale,
Dark faces pale against that rosy flame,
The mild-eyed, melancholy Lotos-eaters came.

Branches they bore of that enchanted stem
Laden with flower and fruit, whereof they gave
To each ; but whoso did receive of them
And taste, to him the gushing of the wave
Far, far away did seem to mourn and rave
On alien shores ; and if his fellow spake,
His voice was thin as voices from the grave ;
And deep-asleep he seemed, yet all awake,
And music in his ears his beating heart did make.

They sat them down upon the yellow sand,
Between the sun and moon, upon the shore ;
And sweet it was to dream of Fatherland,
Of child, and wife, and slave ; — but evermore

Most weary seemed the sea, weary the oar,
Weary the wandering fields of barren foam.
Then some one said, " We will return no more,"
And all at once they sang, " Our island-home
Is far beyond the wave ; we will no longer roam."

ALFRED TENNYSON.

SAPPHO.

SHE lay among the myrtles on the cliff ;
    Above her glared the noon ; beneath, the sea.
Upon the white horizon Athos' peak
Weltered in burning haze ; all airs were dead ;
The cicale slept among the tamarisk's hair ;
The birds sat dumb and drooping. Far below
The lazy sea-weed glistened in the sun ;
The lazy sea-fowl dried their steaming wings ;
The lazy swell crept whispering up the ledge,
And sank again. Great Pan was laid to rest ;
And Mother Earth watched by him as he slept,
And hushed her myriad children for awhile.
She lay among the myrtles on the cliff ;
And sighed for sleep, for sleep that would not hear,
But left her tossing still ; for night and day
A mighty hunger yearned within her heart,
Till all her veins ran fever, and her cheek,
Her long thin hands, and ivory-channell'd feet,
Were wasted with the wasting of her soul.
Then peevishly she flung her on her face,
And hid her eyeballs from the blinding glare,

And fingered at the grass, and tried to cool
Her crisp hot lips against the crisp hot sward :
And then she raised her head, and upward cast
Wild looks from homeless eyes, whose liquid light
Gleamed out between deep folds of blue-black hair,
As gleam twin lakes between the purple peaks
Of deep Parnassus, at the mournful moon.
Beside her lay her lyre.   She snatched the shell,
And waked wild music from its silver strings ;
Then tossed it sadly by. — " Ah, hush ! " she cries,
" Dead offspring of the tortoise and the mine !
Why mock my discords with thine harmonies ?
Although a thrice-Olympian lot be thine,
Only to echo back in every tone
The moods of nobler natures than thine own."

CHARLES KINGSLEY.

THE FISHERMAN'S HUT.

From Stolle.

" GO, boy, and light the torch ! the night
        Is damp and dark and drear :
Thy father sails from foreign lands,
    His ship must soon be near."

The boy sets fire to the torch,
    And hastens to the strand ;
The storm-wind howls, the rain pours down,
    The torch dies in his hand.

The boy flies homeward : " Mother dear,
   Send me not out again !
·The storm did howl, and the wind did blow,
   And the torch went out in the rain."

"O sailor's blood ! O sailor's blood !
   No sailor's blood art thou !
What cares a brisk young sailor's blood
   How wild the tempests blow ! "

The boy sets fire to the torch,
   He hastens to the shore ;
The tempest howls, the rain pours down,
   The torch goes out once more.

The boy flies home : " O mother dear,
   Send me not to the strand !
There's a white woman sitting there,
   And beckoning with her hand ! "

"O sailor's blood ! O sailor's blood !
   No sailor's blood art thou !
Naught does the brave warm sailor's blood
   For mermaid care, I trow ! "

The boy sets fire to the torch,
   And hastens to the shore ;
The tempest howls, the rain pours down,
   The torch dies yet once more.

The boy flies home : " O mother, go
   Thyself now to the shore !
I hear a voice like father's rise
   Through all the ocean's roar."

The mother quickly lifts the torch,
    And sets the hut on fire ;
The tempest howls, the lurid flame
    Shines brighter, broader, higher.

" What hast thou done ?   O mother, woe !
    Hear'st thou the tempest's roar !
How cold the night, how dark and wild, —
    And we've a home no more."

" O sailor's blood !   O sailor's blood !
    No sailor's blood art thou !
Boy, when no other torch will burn,
    The hut shines well, I trow."

The father safely steers his ship
    Right to the blazing strand,
Weathers the ledges all, and soon
    In safety reached the land.

                                C. T. BROOKS.

COUNT ARNALDOS.

A literal translation in the metre of the original.

WHO had ever such adventure,
        On the waters of the sea,
As had once the Count Arnaldos
On the morning of Saint John ?
He was going to the hawking,
With a falcon on his wrist,

When at sea he saw a galley
Slowly drawing near the land.
All her sails of woven silk were ;
Glistening silk the cordage all ;
And the mariner who steered her
Ever sang so sweet a song
That it held the billows quiet,
And it pacified the wind,
And the fishes rose to listen,
And the birds lit on the mast.
" Galley," sang he, " O my galley,
May God keep thee from all harm,
From all dangers that await thee
On the waters of the sea ;
From the shallows of Almeria,
From Gibraltar's narrow strait,
From the stormy gulf of Leon,
And the false Venetian sea ;
From the sunken reefs of Flanders,
Where the peril is most dire."
Then spake out the Count Arnaldos
(You shall hear the words he said) :
" In the name of God, O seaman,
Sing to me again this song ! "
Then the mariner made answer,
And his answer was but this :
" I can tell this song to no one,
Save to him who sails with me."

COUNT ARNALDOS.

From the Spanish.

I.

WHO had ever such adventure,
  Holy priest or virgin nun,
As befel the Count Arnaldos
  At the rising of the sun ?

II.

On h's wrist the hawk was hooded,
  Forth with hcrn and hound went he.
When he saw a stately galley
  Sailing on the silent sea.

III.

Sail of sattin, mast of cedar ;
  Burnished poop of beaten gold, —
Many a morn you'll hood your falcon,
  Ere you such a bark behold.

IV.

Sails of sattin, masts of cedar,
  Golden poops, may come again ;
But mortal ear no more shall listen
  To yon gray-haired sailor's strain.

V.

Heart may beat, and eye may glisten,
  Faith is strong, and hope is free ;
But mortal ear no more shall listen
  To the song that rules the sea.

VI.

When the gray-haired sailor chanted,
  Every wind was hush'd to sleep, —
Like a virgin's bosom panted
  All the wide reposing deep.

VII.

Bright in beauty rose the star-fish
  From her green cave down below,
Right above the eagle poised him, —
  Holy music charmed them so.

VIII.

" Stately galley ! glorious galley !
  God hath pour'd his grace on thee !
Thou alone may'st scorn the perils
  Of the dread devouring sea !

IX.

" False Almeria's reefs and shallows,
  Black Gibraltar's giant rocks,
Sound and sand-bank, gulf and whirlpool,
  All — my glorious galley mocks ! "

X.

" For the sake of God our maker ! "
  (Count Arnaldos' cry was strong,)
" Old man, let me be partaker
  In the secret of thy song ! "

XI.

" Count Arnaldos ! Count Arnaldos !
    Hearts I read, and thoughts I know ; —
Would'st thou learn the ocean secret,
    In our galley thou must go."

J. G. LOCKHART.

THE SECRET OF THE SEA.

AH ! what pleasant visions haunt me,
    As I gaze upon the sea !
All the old romantic legends,
    All my dreams come back to me.

Sails of silk and ropes of sendal,
    Such as gleam in ancient lore ;
And the singing of the sailors,
    And the answer from the shore !

Most of all, the Spanish ballad
    Haunts me oft, and tarries long,
Of the noble Count Arnaldos
    And the sailor's mystic song.

Like the long waves on a sea-beach,
    Where the sand as silver shines,
With a soft, monotonous cadence,
    Flow its unrhymed lyric lines : —

Telling how the Count Arnaldoṡ,
   With his hawk upon his hand,
Saw a fair and stately galley,
   Steering onward to the land ; —

How he heard the ancient helmsman
   Chant a song so wild and clear,
That the sailing sea-bird slowly
   Poised upon the mast to hear,

Till his soul was full of longing,
   And he cried, with impulse strong, —
" Helmsman ! for the love of heaven,
   Teach me, too, that wondrous song ! "

" Would'st thou," so the helmsman answered,
   " Learn the secret of the sea ?
Only those who brave its dangers
   Comprehend its mystery ! "

In each sail that skims the horizon,
   In each landward-blowing breeze,
I behold that stately galley,
   Hear those mournful melodies ;

Till my soul is full of longing
   For the secret of the sea,
And the heart of the great ocean
   Sends a thrilling pulse through me.

                       HENRY W. LONGFELLOW.

FAR, FAR AWAY, ACROSS THE SEA.

Theodore Aubenel.

FAR, far away, across the sea,
    In the still hours when I sit dreaming,
Often and often I voyage in seeming,
And sad is the heart I bear with me
Far, far away, across the sea.

Yonder toward the Dardanelles,
I follow the vessels disappearing,
Slender masts to the sky uprearing.
Follow her, whom I love so well,
Yonder toward the Dardanelles.

With the great clouds I go astray, —
These by the shepherd-wind are driven
Across the shining stars of heaven,
In snowy flocks, and go their way,
And with the clouds I go astray.

I take the pinions of the swallow,
For the fair weather ever yearning,
And swiftly to the sun returning,
So swiftly I my darling follow
Upon the pinions of the swallow.

Home-sickness hath my heart possessed,
For now she treads an alien strand,
And for that unknown fatherland
I long as a bird for her nest.
Home-sickness hath my heart possessed.

From wave to wave the salt sea over,
Like a pale corpse I alway seem,
On-floating in a deathlike dream,
Even to the feet of my sweet lover,
From wave to wave the salt sea over.

Now I am lying on the shore,
Till my love lifts me mutely weeping,
And takes me in her tender keeping,
And lays her hand my still heart o'er,
And calls me from the dead once more.

H. W. P.

THE KING OF THULE.

Goethe.

THERE was a king in Thule
Was faithful till the grave, —
To whom his mistress, dying,
A golden goblet gave.

Naught was to him more precious ;
He drained it at every bout :
His eyes with tears ran over,
As oft as he drank thereout.

When came his time of dying,
The towns in his land he told,
Naught else to his heir denying
Except the goblet of gold.

He sat at the royal banquet
With his knights of high degree,
In the lofty hall of his fathers,
In the castle by the sea.

There stood the old carouser,
And drank the last life glow ;
And hurled the hallowed goblet
Into the tide below.

He saw it plunging and filling,
And sinking deep in the sea :
Then fell his eyelids forever,
And never more drank he.

BAYARD TAYLOR.

THE SWALLOW.

F. Grossi.

SWALLOW from beyond the sea!
  That, with every dawning day,
Sitting on the balcony,
  Utterest that plaintive lay,
What is that thou tellest me
Swallow from beyond the sea?

Haply thou for him who went
  From thee and forgot his mate
Dost lament to my lament,
  Widowed, lonely, desolate.
Even then lament with me,
Swallow from beyond the sea !

Happier yet art thou than I :
　　Thee thy trusty wings may bear,
Over lake and cliff to fly,
　　Filling with thy cries the air,
Calling him continually,
Swallow from beyond the sea !

Could I too ! — but I must pine
　　In this dungeon dark and low,
Where the sun can never shine,
　　Where the breeze can never blow,
Whence my voice scarce reaches thee,
Swallow from beyond the sea !

Now September days are near,
　　Thou to distant lands wilt fly ;
In another hemisphere
　　Other streams shall hear thy cry,
Other hills shall answer thee,
Swallow from beyond the sea !

Then shall I, when daylight grows,
　　Waking to the sense of pain,
'Mid the wintry frosts and snows
　　Think I hear thy notes again, —
Notes that seem to grieve for me,
Swallow from beyond the sea !

Planted here upon the ground,
　　Thou shalt find a cross in spring ·

There, as evening gathers round,
  Swallow, come and rest thy wing;
Chant à strain of peace to me,
Swallow from beyond the sea!

WILLIAM CULLEN BRYANT.

THE SEA.

From the German.

O SEA, in evening's glow,
  Upon thy tranquil breast,
After long storm and woe
  I breathe a heavenly rest.

Thy troubled heart forgets
  The weary war of yore,
Its moans and drear regrets
  Are melody once more.

Barely one voiceless thought
  May through the spirit float,
As on the silent sea
  A solitary boat.

M. C. PIKE.

KING CHRISTIAN.

A national song of Denmark. By Ewald.

KING Christian stood by the lofty mast
  In mist and smoke;
His sword was hammering so fast,
Through Gothic helm and brain it passed;
Then sank each hostile hulk and mast,

In mist and smoke.
" Fly !" shouted they, "fly, he who can !
Who braves of Denmark's Christian
        The stroke?"

Nils Juel gave heed to the tempest's roar,
        Now is the hour !
He hoisted his blood-red flag once more,
And smote upon the foe full sore,
And shouted loud, through the tempest's roar,
        "Now is the hour !"
"Fly !" shouted they, "for shelter fly !
Of Denmark's Juel who can defy
        The power?"

North Sea! a glimpse of Wessel rent
        Thy murky sky !
Then champions to thine arms were sent ;
Terror and Death glared where he went,
From the waves was heard a wail, that rent
        Thy murky sky !
From Denmark, thunders Tordenskiol' ;
Let each to Heaven commend his soul,
        And fly !

Path of the Dane to fame and might !
        Dark-rolling wave !
Receive thy friend, who, scorning flight,
Goes to meet danger with despite,
Proudly as thou the tempest's might,

Dark-rolling wave !
And amid pleasures and alarms,
And war and victory, be thine arms
My grave !

H. W. LONGFELLOW.

BALLAD.

A.D. 1400.

I.

IT was Earl Haldan's daughter,
    She looked across the sea ;
She looked across the water,
And long and loud laughed she :   .
"The locks of six princesses
Must be my marriage fee :
So, hey, bonny boat, and ho, bonny boat,
    Who comes a-wooing me ! "

II.

It was Earl Haldan's daughter,
She walked along the sand,
When she was aware of a knight so fair,
Come sailing to the land.
His sails were all of velvet,
His mast of beaten gold,
And " Hey, bonny boat, and ho, bonny boat,
    Who saileth here so bold ? "

III.

" The locks of five princesses
I won beyond the sea ;
I shore their golden tresses
To fringe a cloak for thee.

One handful yet is wanting,
But one of all the tale ;
So, hey, bonny boat, and ho, bonny boat,
Furl up thy velvet sail ! "

IV.

He leapt into the water,
That rover young and bold ;
He gript Earl Haldan's daughter,
He shore her locks of gold :
" Go weep, go weep, proud maiden,
The tale is full to-day.
Now, hey, bonny boat, and ho, bonny boat,
Sail Westward ho, and away ! "

CHARLES KINGSLEY.

THE WATER-MAN.

An old Danish ballad.

" O MOTHER, rede me well, I pray,
How shall I woo me yon winsome May ? "

She has built him a horse of the water clear,
The saddle and bridle of sea-sand were.

He has donned the garb of a knight so gay,
And to Mary's kirk he has ridden away.

He tied his steed to the chancel door,
And he stepped round the kirk three times and four.

He has boune him into the kirk, and all
Drew near to gaze on him, great and small.

The priest he was standing in the quire : —
"What gay young gallant comes branking here ? "

The winsome maid, to herself said she,
"Oh, were that gay young gallant for me ! "

He stepped o'er one stool, he stepped o'er two :
" O maiden, plight me thine oath so true ! "

He stepped o'er three stools, he stepped o'er four :
" Wilt be mine, sweet May, for evermore ? "

She gave him her hand of the drifted snow :
" Here hast thou my troth, and with thee I'll go."

They went from the kirk with the bridal train ;
They danced in glee, and they danced full fain ;

They danced them down to the salt-sea strand,
And they left them standing there, hand in hand.

" Now wait thee, love, with my steed so free,
And the bonniest bark I'll bring for thee."

And when they passed to the white, white sand,
The ships came sailing on to the land ;

But when they were out in the midst of the sound,
Down went they all in the deep profound !

Long, long on the shore, when the winds were high,
They heard from the waters the maiden's cry.

I rede ye, damsels, as best I can,
Tread not the dance with the Water-man !

THEODORE MARTIN.

SWEET WILLIAM'S FAREWELL TO BLACK-EYED SUSAN.

ALL in the Downs the fleet was moored,
 The streamers waving in the wind,
When black-eyed Susan came aboard.
 " Oh, where shall I my true-love find ?
Tell me, ye jovial sailors, tell me true,
If my sweet William sails among your crew."

William, who high upon the yard
 Rocked with the billows to and fro,
Soon as her well-known voice he heard,
 He sighed and cast his eyes below;
The cord slides swiftly through his glowing hands,
And quick as lightning on the deck he stands.

So the sweet lark, high poised in air,
 Shuts close his pinions to his breast,
If chance his mate's shrill call he hear,
 And drops at once into her nest.
The noblest captain in the British fleet
Might envy William's lip those kisses sweet.

" O Susan, Susan, lovely dear,
 My vows shall ever true remain ;
Let me kiss off that falling tear ;
 We only part to meet again.
Change as ye list, ye winds : my heart shall be
The faithful compass that still points to thee.

" Believe not what the landsmen say,
    Who tempt with doubts thy constant mind :
They'll tell thee sailors when away
    In every port a mistress find.
Yes, yes, believe them when they tell thee so,
For thou art present wheresoe'er I go.

" If to fair India's coast we sail,
    Thy eyes are seen in diamonds bright,
Thy breath is Afric's spicy gale,
    Thy skin is ivory so white.
Thus every beauteous object that I view
Wakes in my soul some charm of lovely Sue.

"Though battle call me from thy arms,
    Let not my pretty Susan mourn ;
Though cannons roar, yet safe from harms
    William shall to his dear return.
Love turns aside the balls that round me fly,
Lest precious tears should drop from Susan's eye."

The boatswain gave the dreadful word,
    The sails their swelling bosom spread ;
No longer must she stay aboard ;
    They kissed, she sighed, he hung his head.
Her lessening boat unwilling rows to land :
" Adieu ! " she cries, and waved her lily hand.

                                        JOHN GAY.

THE BALLAD OF THE BOAT.

THE stream was smooth as glass ; we said, " Arise,
    and let's away ! "
The Siren sang beside the boat that in the rushes lay ;
And spread the sail and strong the oar, we gayly took
    our way.
When shall the sandy bar be crossed ? when shall we
    find the bay ?

The broadening flood swells slowly out o'er cattle-
    dotted plains,
The stream is strong and turbulent, and dark with
    heavy rains ;
The laborer looks up to see our shallop speed away.
When shall the sandy bar be crossed ? when shall we
    find the bay ?

Now are the clouds like fiery shrouds ; the sun, su-
    perbly large,
Slow as an oak to woodman's stroke, sinks flaming at
    their marge ;
The waves are bright with mirrored light as jacinths
    on our way.
When shall the sandy bar be crossed ? when shall we
    find the bay ?

The moon is high up in the sky, and now no more we
    see
The spreading river's either bank, and surging dis-
    tantly

There booms a sullen thunder, as of breakers far away.
Now shall the sandy bar be crossed, now shall we find
the bay !

The sea-gull shrieks high overhead, and dimly to our
sight
The moonlit crests of foaming waves gleam towering
through the night.
We'll steal upon the mermaid soon, and start her from
her lay,
When once the sandy bar is crossed, and we are in the
bay.

What rises white and awful as a shroud-enfolded
ghost?
What roar of rampant tumult bursts in clangor on the
coast?
Pull back! pull back! The raging flood sweeps every
oar away.
O stream, is this thy bar of sand? O boat, is this the
bay?

R. GARRETT.

THE SEA-MAID.

A MAIDEN came gliding o'er the sea,
    In a boat as light as boat could be;
And she sang in tones so sweet and free,
" Oh, where is the youth that will follow me?"

Her forehead was white as the pearly shell,
And in flickering waves her ringlets fell,
Her bosom heaved with a gentle swell,
And her voice was a distant vesper bell.

And still she sang, while the western light
Fell on her figure so soft and bright,
" Oh, where shall I find the brave young sprite
That will follow the track of my skiff to-night ? "

To the strand the youths of the village run,
When the witching song has scarce begun,
And ere the set of that evening sun
Fifteen bold lovers the maid has won.

They hoisted the sail, and they plied the oar,
And away they went from their native shore,
While the damsel's pinnace flew fast before,
But never, O never we saw them more !

JOHN STERLING.

THE LANDING OF THE PILGRIM
FATHERS.

THE breaking waves dashed high
    On a stern and rock-bound coast,
And the woods against a stormy sky
    Their giant branches tossed;

And the heavy night hung dark
    The hills and waters o'er,
When a band of exiles moored their bark
    On the wild New England shore.

Not as the conqueror comes,
  They, the true-hearted, came, —
Not with the roll of the stirring drums,
  And the trumpet that sings of fame ;

Not as the flying come,
  In silence and in fear, —
They shook the depths of the desert gloom
  With their hymns of lofty cheer.

Amidst the storm they sang,
  And the stars heard, and the sea ;
And the sounding aisles of the dim woods rang
  To the anthem of the free.

The ocean-eagle soared
  From his nest by the white wave's foam,
And the rocking pines of the forest roared, —
  This was their welcome home.

There were men with hoary hair
  Amidst that pilgrim band ;
Why had they come to wither there,
  Away from their childhood's land ?

There was woman's fearless eye,
  Lit by her deep love's truth ;
There was manhood's brow serenely high,
  And the fiery heart of youth.

What sought they thus afar ?
  Bright jewels of the mine ?
The wealth of seas, the spoils of war ? —
  They sought a faith's pure shrine !

Ay, call it holy ground,
  The soil where first they trod ; —
They have left unstained what there they found, —
  Freedom to worship God.

FELICIA HEMANS.

" The sad rhyme of the men who proudly clung
To their first fault, and withered in their pride."

From Paracelsus.

OVER the sea our galleys went,
    With cleaving prows in order brave,
To a speeding wind and a bounding wave, —
    A gallant armament :
Each bark built out of a forest tree,
Left leafy and rough as first it grew,
And nailed all over the gaping sides,
Within and without, with black-bull hides,
Seethed in fat and suppled in flame,
To bear the playful billows' game.
So each good ship was rude to see,
Rude and bare to the outward view,
    But each upbore a stately tent ;
Where cedar pales in scented row
Kept out the flakes of the dancing brine :
And an awning drooped the mast below,
In fold on fold of the purple fine,
That neither noon-tide, nor star-shine,
Nor moonlight cold which maketh mad,
    Might pierce the regal tenement.

When the sun dawned, oh, gay and glad
We set the sail and plied the oar ;
But when the night-wind blew like breath,
For joy of one day's voyage more,
We sang together on the wide sea,
Like men at peace on a peaceful shore ;
Each sail was loosed to the wind so free,
Each helm made sure by the twilight star,
And in a sleep as calm as death,
We, the strangers from afar,
　　　Lay stretched along, each weary crew
In a circle round its wondrous tent,
Whence gleamed soft light and curled rich scent,
　　　And, with light and perfume, music too :
So the stars wheeled round, and the darkness past,
And at morn we started beside the mast,
And still each ship was sailing fast !

One morn the land appeared ! — a speck
Dim trembling betwixt sea and sky.
" Avoid it," cried our pilot, " check
　　　The shout, restrain the longing eye ! "
But the heaving sea was black behind
For many a night and many a day,
And land, though but a rock, drew nigh ;
So we broke the cedar pales away,
Let the purple awning flap in the wind,
　　　And a statue bright was on every deck !
We shouted, every man of us,
And steered right into the harbor thus,
With pomp and pæan glorious.

An hundred shapes of lucid stone !
 All day we built a shrine for each, —
A shrine of rock for every one, —
Nor paused we, till in the westering sun
 We sate together on the beach
To sing, because our task was done ;
When lo ! what shouts and merry songs !
What laughter all the distance stirs !
What raft comes loaded with its throngs
Of gentle islanders ?
 " The isles are just at hand," they cried ;
  " Like cloudlets faint at even sleeping,
 Our temple-gates are opened wide,
  Our olive-groves thick shade are keeping
 For the lucid shapes you bring," they cried.
Oh, then we awoke with sudden start
From our deep dream ; we knew, too late,
How bare the rock, how desolate,
To which we had flung our precious freight :
 Yet we called out, " Depart !
  Our gifts, once given, must here abide :
 Our work is done ; we have no heart
  To mar our work, though vain," we cried.

ROBERT BROWNING.

HERVÉ RIEL.

ON the sea and at the Hogue, sixteen hundred
    ninety-two,
Did the English fight the French, — woe to France!
And the thirty-first of May, helter-skelter through the
    blue,
Like a crowd of frightened porpoises a shoal of sharks
    pursue,
    Came crowding ship on ship to St. Malo on the
     Rance,
With the English fleet in view.

'Twas the squadron that escaped, with the victor in
    full chase:
    First and foremost of the drove, in his great ship,
     Damfreville;
    Close on him fled, great and small,
    Twenty-two good ships in all;
And they signalled to the place,
" Help the winners of a race!
    Get us guidance, give us harbor, take us quick; or,
     quicker still,
    Here's the English can and will!"

Then the pilots of the place put out brisk, and leaped on
    board:
    " Why, what hope or chance have ships like these to
     pass?" laughed they:

Rocks to starboard, rocks to port, all the passage
    scarred and scored,
Shall the ' Formidable,' here, with her twelve and eighty
    guns,
  Think to make the river-mouth by the single narrow
    way,
Trust to enter where 'tis ticklish for a craft of twenty
    tons,
    And with flow at full beside ?
    Now 'tis slackest ebb of tide.
  Reach the mooring ?   Rather say,
While rock stands, or water runs,
    Not a ship will leave the bay ! "

Then was called a council straight :
Brief and bitter the debate.
" Here's the English at our heels : would you have
    them take in tow
All that's left us of the fleet, linked together stern and
    bow,
For a prize to Plymouth sound ?
Better run the ships aground ! "
    (Ended Damfreville his speech.)
" Not a minute more to wait !
    Let the captains all and each
    Shove ashore, then blow up, burn the vessels on the
    beach !
France must undergo her fate ! "

" Give the word ! "   But no such word
Was ever spoke or heard :
    For up stood, for out stepped, for in struck, amid all
    these, —

A captain ? a lieutenant ? a mate, — first, second, third ?
   No such man of mark, and meet
   With his betters to compete !
   But a simple Breton sailor, pressed by Tourville
     for the fleet,
  A poor coasting-pilot he, — Hervé Riel the Croisick-
   ese.

And " What mockery or malice have we here ? " cried
   Hervé Riel.
  " Are you mad, you Malouins ?   Are you cowards,
    fools, or rogues ?
Talk to me of rocks and shoals ? — me, who took the
   soundings, tell
On my fingers every bank, every shallow, every swell,
  'Twixt the offing here and Grève, where the river
   disembogues ?
Are you bought for English gold? Is it love the
   lying's for ?
   Morn and eve, night and day,
   Have I piloted your bay,
Entered free and anchored fast at the foot of Solidor.
  Burn the fleet, and ruin France? That were worse
    than fifty Hogues !
   Sirs, they know I speak the truth ! Sirs, believe
    me, there's a way !
Only let me lead the line,
  Have the biggest ship to steer,
  Get this ' Formidable ' clear,
Make the others follow mine,
And I lead them, most and least, by a passage I know
   well,

Right to Solidor past Grève,
    And there lay them safe and sound ;
And, if one ship misbehave, —
    Keel so much as grate the ground, —
Why, I've nothing but my life : here's my head ! " cries
    Hervé Riel.

Not a minute more to wait.
" Steer us in, then, small and great !
    Take the helm, lead the line, save the squadron ! "
    cried its chief.
Captains, give the sailor place !
    He is admiral, in brief.
Still the north-wind, by God's grace.
See the noble fellow's face,
As the big ship, with a bound,
Clears the entry like a hound,
Keeps the passage, as its inch of way were the wide
    sea's profound !
    See, safe through shoal and rock,
    How they follow in a flock ;
Not a ship that misbehaves, not a keel that grates the
    ground,
    Not a spar that comes to grief !
The peril, see, is past !
All are harbored to the last !
And, just as Hervé Riel hollas " Anchor ! " sure as
    fate,
Up the English come, — too late !

So the storm subsides to calm :
    They see the green trees wave

On the heights o'erlooking Grève ;
Hearts that bled are stanched with balm.
" Just our rapture to enhance,
   Let the English rake the bay,
Gnash their teeth, and glare askance
   As they cannonade away !
'Neath rampired Solidor pleasant riding on the
     Rance ! "
How hope succeeds despair on each captain's coun-
     tenance !
Out burst all with one accord,
  " This is paradise for hell !
    Let France, let France's king,
    Thank the man that did the thing ! "
What a shout, and all one word,
  " Hervé Riel ! "
As he stepped in front once more ;
   Not a symptom of surprise
   In the frank blue Breton eyes, —
Just the same man as before.

Then said Damfreville, " My friend,
I must speak out at the end,
   Though I find the speaking hard :
Praise is deeper than the lips :
You have saved the king his ships ;
   You must name your own reward.
'Faith, our sun was near eclipse !
Demand whate'er you will,
France remains your debtor still.
Ask to heart's content, and have ! or my name's not
     Damfreville."

Then a beam of fun outbroke
On the bearded mouth that spoke,
As the honest heart laughed through
Those frank eyes of Breton blue : —
" Since I needs must say my say ;
   Since on board the duty's done,
   And from Malo Roads to Croisic Point what is it
      but a run ? —
Since 'tis ask and have, I may ;
   Since the others go ashore, —
Come ! A good whole holiday !
   Leave to go and see my wife, whom I call the Belle
      Aurore ! "
   That he asked, and that he got, — nothing more.

Name and deed alike are lost :
Not a pillar nor a post
   In his Croisic keeps alive the feat as it befell ;
Not a head in white and black
On a single fishing-smack
In memory of the man but for whom had gone to
      wrack
   All that France saved from the fight whence England
      bore the bell.
Go to Paris ; rank on rank
   Search the heroes flung pell-mell
On the Louvre, face and flank :
   You shall look long enough ere you come to Hervé
      Riel.
So, for better and for worse,
Hervé Riel, accept my verse !

In my verse, Hervé Riel, do thou once more
Save the squadron, honor France, love thy wife the
   Belle Aurore !

ROBERT BROWNING.

THE "GRAY SWAN."

" OH, tell me, sailor, tell me true,
   Is my little lad, my Elihu,
A-sailing with your ship ? "
The sailor's eyes were dim with dew.
" Your little lad, your Elihu ? "
   He said with trembling lip, —
   " What little lad ? what ship ? "

" What little lad ? as if there could be
Another such a one as he !
   What little lad, do you say ?
Why, Elihu, that took to the sea
The moment I put him off my knee !
   It was just the other day
   The ' Gray Swan ' sailed away."

" The other day ? " The sailor's eyes
Stood open with a great surprise :
   " The other day ? the ' Swan ' ? "
His heart began in his throat to rise.
" Ay, ay, sir, here in the cupboard lies
   The jacket he had on."
   " And so your lad is gone ? "

"Gone with the 'Swan'?"—"And did she stand
With her anchor clutching hold of the sand
   For a month, and never stir?"
"Why, to be sure! I've seen from the land,
Like a lover kissing his lady's hand,
   The wild sea kissing her,—
   A sight to remember, sir!"

"But, my good mother, do you know
All this was twenty years ago?
   I stood on the 'Gray Swan's' deck,
And to that lad I saw you throw,
Taking it off as it might be,—so!—
   The kerchief from your neck."
   "Ay, and he'll bring it back!"

"And did the little lawless lad,
That has made you sick and made you sad,
   Sail with the 'Gray Swan's' crew?"
"Lawless! The man is going mad!
The best boy ever mother had!—
   Be sure he sailed with the crew!
   What would you have him do?"

"And has he never written line,
Nor sent you word, nor made you sign,
   To say he was alive?"
"Hold! If 'twas wrong, the wrong is mine;
Besides, he may lie in the brine;
   And could he write from the grave?
   Tut, man! what would you have?"

" Gone twenty years, — a long, long cruise!
'Twas wicked thus your love to abuse!
    But if the lad still live,
And come back home, think you you can
Forgive him ? " — " Miserable man !
    You're mad as the sea, you rave !
    What have I to forgive ?"

The sailor twitched his shirt so blue,
And from within his bosom drew
    The kerchief.   She was wild.
"O God, my Father! is it true ?
My little lad, my Elihu !
    My blessed boy, my child !
    My dead, my living child!"

ALICE CARY.

THE PHANTOM SHIP.

IN Mather's "Magnalia Christi,"
    Of the old colonial time,
May be found in prose the legend
    That is here set down in rhyme.

A ship sailed from New Haven,
    And the keen and frosty airs,
That filled her sails at parting,
    Were heavy with good men's prayers.

" O Lord ! if it be thy pleasure " —
    Thus prayed the old divine —
"To bury our friends in the ocean,
    Take them, for they are thine !"

But Master Lamberton muttered,
  And under his breath said he,
" This ship is so crank and walty,
  I fear our grave she will be ! "

And the ships that came from England,
  When the winter months were gone,
Brought no tidings of this vessel,
  Nor of Master Lamberton.

This put the people to praying
  That the Lord would let them hear
What in his greater wisdom
  He had done with friends so dear.

And at last their prayers were answered :
  It was in the month of June,
An hour before the sunset
  Of a windy afternoon,

When, steadily steering landward,
  A ship was seen below,
And they knew it was Lamberton, Master,
  Who sailed so long ago.

On she came, with a cloud of canvas,
  Right against the wind that blew,
Until the eye could distinguish
  The faces of the crew.

Then fell her straining topmasts,
  Hanging tangled in the shrouds,
And her sails were loosened and lifted,
  And blown away like clouds.

And their masts, with all their rigging,
  Fell slowly, one by one,
And the hulk dilated and vanished,
  As a sea-mist in the sun !   .

And the people who saw this marvel
  Each said unto his friend,
That this was the mould of their vessel,
  And thus her tragic end.

And the pastor of the village
  Gave thanks to God in prayer,
That, to quiet their troubled spirits,
  He had sent this Ship of Air.

HENRY W. LONGFELLOW.

THE FORSAKEN MERMAN.

COME, dear children, let us away !
    Down and away below.
Now my brothers call from the bay ;
Now the great winds shorewards blow ;
Now the salt tides seawards flow ;
Now the wild white horses play,
Champ and chaff and toss in the spray.
    Children dear, let us away ;
    This way, this way.

Call her once before you go.
    Call once yet,

In a voice that she will know:
      " Margaret ! Margaret ! "
Children's voices should be dear
(Call once more) to a mother's ear ;
Children's voices wild with pain.
      Surely she will come again.
Call her once, and come away ;
      This way, this way.
" Mother dear, we cannot stay,"
The wild white horses foam and fret,
      Margaret ! Margaret !

Come, dear children, come away down.
      Call no more.
One last look at the white-walled town,
And the little gray church on the windy shore,
      Then come down.
She will not come, though you call all day.
      Come away, come away.

Children dear, was it yesterday
We heard the sweet bells over the bay ;
      In the caverns where we lay,
      Through the surf and through the swell,
The far-off sound of a silver bell ?
Sand-strewn caverns cool and deep,
Where the winds are all asleep ;
Where the spent lights quiver and gleam ;
Where the salt weed sways in the stream ;
Where the sea-beasts, ranged all round,
Feed in the ooze of their pasture-ground ;

Where the sea-snakes coil and twine,
Dry their mail, and bask in the brine ;
Where great whales come sailing by,
Sail and sail, with unshut eye,
Round the world for ever and aye ?
   When did music come this way?
   Children dear, was it yesterday ?
Children dear, was it yesterday
(Call yet once) that she went away ?
Once she sat with you and me,
   On a red gold throne in the heart of the sea,
   And the youngest sat on her knee.
She combed its bright hair and she tended it well,
When down swung the sound of the far-off bell ;
She sighed, she looked up through the clear green sea ;
She said, " I must go, for my kinsfolk pray
In the little gray church on the shore to-day.
'Twill be Easter-time in the world — ah me !
And I lose my poor soul, merman, here with thee."
I said, " Go up, dear heart, through the waves ;
Say thy prayer, and come back to the kind sea-caves."
She smiled, she went up through the surf in the bay ;
   Children dear, was it yesterday ?

   Children dear, were we long alone ?
" The sea grows stormy, the little ones moan ;
Long prayers," I said, " in the world they say.
Come," I said, and we rose through the surf in the
   bay.
We went up the beach in the sandy down
Where the sea-stocks bloom, to the white-walled town,

Through the narrow-paved streets where all was still,
To the little gray church on the windy hill.
From the church came a murmur of folk at their
      prayers,
But we stood without in the cold blowing airs,
We climbed on the graves, on the stones worn with
      rains,
And we gazed up the aisle through the small leaded
      panes.
      She sat by the pillar ; we saw her clear ;
      " Margaret, hist ! come quick, we are here.
      Dear heart," I said, " we are here alone ;
      The sea grows stormy, the little ones moan."
But ah ! she gave me never a look,
For her eyes were sealed to the holy book.
      " Loud prays the priest ; shut stands the door,"
Come away, children, call no more,
Come away, come down, call no more.

      Down, down, down,
      Down to the depths of the sea ;
She sits at her wheel in the humming town,
      Singing most joyfully.
Hark what she sings : " O joy, O joy,
For the humming street, and the child with its toy,
For the priest and the bell, and the holy well,
      For the wheel where I spun,
      And the blessed light of the sun."
And so she sings her fill,
      Singing most joyfully,
      Till the shuttle falls from her hand,
      And the whizzing wheel stands still.

She steals to the window and looks at the sand ;
  And over the sand at the sea ;
  And her eyes are set in a stare ;
  And anon there breaks a sigh,
  And anon there drops a tear,
  From a sorrow-clouded eye,
  And a heart sorrow-laden,
   A long, long sigh,
For the cold strange eyes of a little mermaiden,
And the gleam of her golden hair.

  Come away, away, children,
  Come, children, come down.
  The hoarse wind blows colder ;
  Lights shine in the town.
  She will start from her slumber
  When gusts shake the door ;
  She will hear the winds howling,
  Will hear the waves roar ;
  We shall see, while above us
  The waves roar and whirl,
  A ceiling of amber,
  A pavement of pearl.
  Singing, " Here came a mortal,
  But faithless was she,
  And alone dwell for ever
  The kings of the sea."

  But children, at midnight,
  When soft the winds blow,
  When clear falls the moonlight,
  When spring-tides are low,

When sweet airs come seaward
From heaths starred with broom,
And high rocks throw mildly
On the blanched sands a gloom ;
Up the still, glistening beaches,
Up the creeks we will hie ;
Over banks of bright seaweed
The ebb-tide leaves dry.
We will gaze from the sand-hills,
At the white sleeping town ;
At the church on the hill-side, —
    And then come back, down.
Singing, "There dwells a loved one,
    But cruel is she ;
    She left lonely for ever
    The kings of the sea."

MATTHEW ARNOLD.

THE DEAD SHIP OF HARPSWELL.

WHAT flecks the outer gray beyond
    The sundown's golden trail ?
The white flash of a sea-bird's wing,
    Or gleam of slanting sail ?
Let young eyes watch from Neck and Point,
    And sea-worn elders pray, —
The ghost of what was once a ship
    Is sailing up the bay !

From gray sea-fog, from icy drift,
    From peril and from pain,
The home-bound fisher greets thy lights,
    O hundred-harbored Maine !
But many a keel shall seaward turn,
    And many a sail outstand,
When, tall and white, the Dead Ship looms
    Against the dusk of land.

She rounds the headland's briśtling pines ;
    She threads the isle-set bay ;
No spur of breeze can speed her on,
    Nor ebb of tide delay.
Old men still walk the Isle of Orr
    Who tell her date and name ;
Old shipwrights sit in Freeport yards
    Who hewed her oaken frame.

What weary doom of baffled quest,
    Thou sad sea-ghost, is thine ?
What makes thee in the haunts of home
    A wonder and a sign ?
No foot is on thy silent deck,
    Upon thy helm no hand ;
No ripple hath the soundless wind
    That smites thee from the land !

For never comes the ship to port,
    Howe'er the breeze may be ;
Just when she nears the waiting shore, ·
    She drifts again to sea.

No tack of sail, nor turn of helm,
    Nor sheer of veering side ;
Stern-fore she drives to sea and night,
    Against the wind and tide.

In vain o'er Harpswell Neck the star
    Of evening guides her in ;
In vain for her the lamps are lit
    Within thy tower, Seguin !
In vain the harbor-boat shall hail,
    In vain the pilot call ;
No hand shall reef her spectral sail,
    Or let her anchor fall.

Shake, brown old wives, with dreary joy,
    Your gray-head hints of ill ;
And, over sick-beds whispering low,
    Your prophecies fulfil.
Some home amid yon birchen trees
    Shall drape its door with woe ;
And slowly where the Dead Ship sails
    The burial-boat shall row !

From Wolf Neck and from Flying Point,
    From island and from main,
From sheltered cove and tided creek,
    Shall glide the funeral train.
The dead-boat with the bearers four,
    The mourners at her stern, —
And one shall go the silent way
    Who shall no more return !

And men shall sigh, and women weep,
   Whose dear ones pale and pine,
And sadly over sunset seas
   Await the ghostly sign.
They know not that its sails are filled
   By pity's tender breath,
Nor see the Angel at the helm
   Who steers the Ship of Death!

JOHN GREENLEAF WHITTIER.

THE "THREE BELLS."

BENEATH the low-hung night cloud
   That raked her splintering mast,
The good ship settled slowly,
   The cruel leak gained fast.

Over the awful ocean
   Her signal guns pealed out.
Dear God! was that thy answer
   From the horror round about?

A voice came down the wild wind,
   "Ho! ship ahoy!" its cry:
"Our stout 'Three Bells' of Glasgow
   Shall lay till daylight by!"

Hour after hour crept slowly,
   Yet on the heaving swells
Tossed up and down the ship-lights,
   The lights of the "Three Bells"!

And ship to ship made signals,
   Man answered back to man,
While oft, to cheer and hearten,
   The " Three Bells " nearer ran ;

And the captain from her taffrail
   Sent down his hopeful cry.
" Take heart ! Hold on ! " he shouted,
   " The ' Three Bells ' shall lay by ! "

All night across the waters
   The tossing lights shone clear ;
All night from reeling taffrail
   The " Three Bells " sent her cheer.

And when the dreary watches
   Of storm and darkness passed,
Just as the wreck lurched under,
   All souls were saved at last.

Sail on, " Three Bells," for ever,
   In grateful memory sail !
Ring on, " Three Bells," of rescue,
   Above the wave and gale !

Type of the Love eternal,
   Repeat the Master's cry,
As, tossing through our darkness,
   The lights of God draw nigh !

JOHN GREENLEAF WHITTIER.

SKIPPER IRESON'S RIDE.

OF all the rides since the birth of time,
  Told in story or sung in rhyme, —
On Apuleius's Golden Ass,
Or one-eyed Calendar's horse of brass,
Witch astride on a human hack,
Islam's prophet on Al Borák, —
The strangest ride that ever was sped
Was Ireson's, out from Marblehead !
  Old Floyd Ireson, for his hard heart,
  Tarred and feathered and carried in a cart
    By the women of Marblehead !

Body of turkey, head of owl,
Wings a-droop like a rained-on fowl,
Feathered and ruffled in every part,
Skipper Ireson stood in the cart.
Scores of women, old and young,
Strong of muscle, and glib of tongue,
Pushed and pulled up the rocky lane,
Shouting and singing the shrill refrain :
  " Here's Flud Oirson, fur his horrd horrt,
  Torr'd an' futherr'd an' corr'd in a corrt,
    By the women o' Morble'ead ! "

Wrinkled scolds with hands on hips,
Girls in bloom of check and lips,
Wild-eyed, free-limbed, such as chase
Bacchus round some antique vase,

Brief of skirt, with ankles bare,
Loose of kerchief and loose of hair,
With conch-shells blowing and fish-horns' twang,
Over and over the Mænads sang:
  " Here's Flud Oirson, fur his horrd horrt,
    Torr'd an' futherr'd an' corr'd in a corrt
      By the women o' Morble'ead ! "

Small pity for him ! — He had sailed away
From a leaking ship, in Chaleur bay, —
Sailed away from a sinking wreck,
With his own town's-people on her deck !
" Lay by ! lay by ! " they called to him.
Back he answered, " Sink or swim !
Brag of your catch of fish again ! "
And off he sailed through the fog and rain !
  Old Floyd Ireson, for his hard heart,
    Tarred and feathered and carried in a cart
      By the women of Marblehead.

Fathoms deep in dark Chaleur
That wreck shall lie for evermore.
Mother and sister, wife and maid,
Looked from the rocks of Marblehead
Over the moaning and rainy sea, —
Looked for the coming that might not be !
What did the winds and the sea-birds say
Of the cruel captain who sailed away ? —
  Old Floyd Ireson, for his hard heart,
    Tarred and feathered and carried in a cart
      By the women of Marblehead !

Through the street, on either side,
Up flew windows, doors swung wide ;
Sharp-tongued spinsters, old wives gray,
Treble lent the fish-horn's bray.
Sea-worn grandsires, cripple-bound,
Hulks of old sailors run aground,
Shook head, and fist, and hat, and cane,
And cracked with curses the hoarse refrain :
  " Here's Flud Oirson, for his horrd horrt,
  Torr'd an' futherr'd an' corr'd in a corrt
    By the women o' Morble'ead ! "

Sweetly along the Salem road
Bloom of orchard and lilac showed.
Little the wicked skipper knew
Of the fields so green and the sky so blue.
Riding there in his sorry trim,
Like an Indian idol glum and grim,
Scarcely he seemed the sound to hear
Of the voices shouting, far and near :
  " Here's Flud Oirson, for his horrd horrt,
  Torr'd an' futherr'd an' corr'd in a corrt
    By the women o' Morble'ead ! "

" Hear me, neighbors ! " at last he cried, —
" What to me is this noisy ride ?
What is the shame that clothes the skin
To the nameless horror that lives within ?
Waking or sleeping, I see a wreck,
And hear a cry from a reeling deck !
Hate me and curse me, — I only dread
The hand of God and the face of the dead ! "

Said old Floyd Ireson, for his hard heart,
Tarred and feathered and carried in a cart
   By the women of Marblehead.

Then the wife of the skipper lost at sea
Said, " God has touched him ! — why should we ? "
Said an old wife mourning her only son,
" Cut the rogue's tether and let him run ! "
So with soft relentings and rude excuse,
Half scorn, half pity, they cut him loose,
And gave him a cloak to hide him in,
And left him alone with his shame and sin.
   Poor Floyd Ireson, for his hard heart,
   Tarred and feathered and carried in a cart
     By the women of Marblehead.

JOHN GREENLEAF WHITTIER.

THE WIVES OF BRIXHAM.

YOU see the gentle water,
   How silently it floats,
How cautiously, how steadily
   It moves the sleepy boats ;
And all the little loops of pearl
   It strews along the sand
Steal out as leisurely as leaves,
   When summer is at hand.

But you know it can be angry,
   And thunder from its rest,
When the stormy taunts of winter
   Are flying at its breast ;

And if you like to listen,
  And draw your chairs around,
I'll tell you what it did one night,
  When you were sleeping sound.

The merry boats of Brixham
  Go out to search the seas, —
A stanch and sturdy fleet are they,
  Who love a swinging breeze ;
And before the woods of Devon,
  And the silver cliffs of Wales,
You may see, when summer evenings fall,
  The light upon their sails.

But when the year grows darker,
  And gray winds hunt the foam,
They go back to little Brixham,
  And ply their toils at home.
And thus it chanced one winter's day,
  When a storm began to roar,
That all the men were out at sea,
  And all the wives on shore.

Then as the wind grew fiercer,
  The women's cheeks grew white, —
It was fercer in the twilight,
  And fiercest in the night.
The strong clouds set themselves like ice,
  Without a star to melt ;
The blackness of the darkness
  Was something to be felt.

The storm, like an assassin,
  Went on its secret way,
And struck a hundred boats adrift
  To reel about the bay.
They meet, they crash, — God keep the men !
  God give a moment's light !
There is nothing but the tumult,
  And the tempest, and the night.

The men on shore were anxious, —
  They grieved for what they knew :
What do you think the women did ?
  Love taught them what to do !
Outspoke a wife : " We've beds at home,
  We'll burn them for a light !
Give us the men and the bare ground !
  We want no more to-night."

They took the grandame's blanket,
  Who shivered and bade them go ;
They took the baby's pillow,
  Who could not say them no ;
And they heaped a great fire on the pier,
  And knew not all the while
If they were heaping a bonfire,
  Or only a funeral pile.

And, fed with precious food, the flame
  Shone bravely on the black,
Till a cry rang through the people, —
  " A boat is coming back ! "

Staggering dimly through the fog,
   They see, and then they doubt;
But, when the first prow strikes the pier,
   Cannot you hear them shout?

Then all along the breadth of flame
   Dark figures shrieked and ran,
With, " Child, here comes your father! "
   Or, " Wife, is this your man? "
And faint feet touch the welcome shore,
   And stay a little while;
And kisses drop from frozen lips,
   Too tired to speak or smile.

So, one by one, they struggled in,
   All that the sea would spare:
We will not reckon through our tears
   The names that were not there;
But some went home without a bed,
   When all the tale was told,
Who were too cold with sorrow
   To know the night was cold.

And this is what the men must do,
   Who work in wind and foam;
And this is what the women bear,
   Who watch for them at home.
So when you see a Brixham boat
   Go out to face the gales,
Think of the love that travels
   Like light upon her sails!

M. B. S.

HANNAH BINDING SHOES.

POOR lone Hannah
    Sitting at the window binding shoes, —
Faded, wrinkled, —
Sitting, stitching in a mournful muse.
    Bright-eyed beauty once was she,
    When the bloom was on the tree.
    Spring and winter
Hannah's at the window binding shoes.

    Not a neighbor
Passing nod or answer will refuse
    To her whisper :
"Is there from the fishers any news ? "
    Oh, her heart's adrift with one
    On an endless voyage gone !
    Night and morning
Hannah's at the window binding shoes.

    Fair young Hannah
Ben, the sunburnt fisher, gayly wooes ;
    Hale and clever,
For a willing heart and hand he sues.
    May-day skies are all aglow,
    And the waves are laughing so !
    For her wedding
Hannah leaves her window and her shoes.

May is passing, —
'Mid the apple-boughs a pigeon cooes.
Hannah shudders,
For the wild sou'wester mischief brews.
Round the rocks of Marblehead,
Outward bound, a schooner sped.
Silent, lonesome,
Hannah's at the window binding shoes.

'Tis November,
Now no tear her wasted cheek bedews.
From Newfoundland
Not a sail returning will she lose ;
Whispering hoarsely, " Fishermen,
Have you, have you heard of Ben ? "
Old with watching,
Hannah's at the window binding shoes.

Twenty winters
Bleach and tear the ragged shore she views.
Twenty seasons : —
Never one has brought her any news.
Still her dim eyes silently
Chase the white sails o'er the sea.
Hopeless, faithful,
Hannah's at the window binding shoes.

Lucy Larcom.

A GREYPORT LEGEND.

1797.

THEY ran through the streets of the seaport town,
  They peered from the decks of the ships that lay ;
The cold sea-fog that came whitening down
  Was never so cold or white as they.
"Ho ! Starbuck, Pinckney, and Tenterden !
Run for your shallops, gather your men,
  Scatter your boats on the lower bay."

Good cause for fear ! In the thick mid-day,
  The hulk that lay by the rotting pier,
Filled with the children in happy play,
  Parted its moorings and drifted clear, —
Drifted clear beyond reach or call, —
Thirteen children they were in all, —
  All adrift in the lower bay !

Said a hard-faced skipper, " God help us all !
  She will not float till the turning tide ! "
Said his wife, " My darling will hear *my* call,
  Whether in sea or heaven she bide."
And she lifted a quavering voice and high,
Wild and strange as the sea-bird's cry,
  Till they shuddered and wondered at her side.

The fog drove down on each laboring crew,
  Veiled each from each, and the sky and shore.
There was not a sound but the breath they drew,
  And the lap of water and creak of oar ;

And they felt the breath of the downs fresh blown
O'er leagues of clover and cold gray stone,
    But not from the lips that had gone before.

They came no more.   But they tell the tale
   That, when fogs are thick on the harbor-reef,
The mackerel fishers shorten sail,
   For the signal they know will bring relief,
For the voices of children still at play
In a phantom hulk that drifts away
    Through channels whose waters never fail.

It is but a foolish shipman's tale,
   A theme for a poet's idle page ;
But still when the mists of doubt prevail,
   And we lie becalmed by the shores of age,
We hear from the misty troubled shore
The voice of the children gone before,
    Drawing the soul to its anchorage.

BRET HARTE

THE JUMBLIES.

From "Nonsense Songs."

I.

THEY went to sea in a sieve, they did ;
   In a sieve they went to sea :
In spite of all their friends could say,
On a winter's morn, on a stormy day,
   In a sieve they went to sea.

And when the sieve turned round and round,
And every one cried, " You'll all be drowned ! "
They called aloud, " Our sieve ain't big :
But we don't care a button ; we don't care a fig ;
    In a sieve we'll go to sea ! "
      Far and few, far and few,
        Are the lands where the Jumblies live :
        Their heads are green, and their hands are blue ;
        And they went to sea in a sieve.

II.

They sailed away in a sieve, they did ;
    In a sieve they sailed so fast,
With only a beautiful pea-green veil,
Tied with a ribbon, by way of a sail,
    To a small tobacco-pipe mast.
And every one said, who saw them go :
" Oh ! won't they be soon upset, you know :
For the sky is dark, and the voyage is long ;
And, happen what may, it's extremely wrong
    In a sieve to sail so fast."
      Far and few, far and few,
        Are the lands where the Jumblies live :
        Their heads are green, and their hands are blue :
        And they went to sea in a sieve.

III.

The water it soon came in, it did ;
    The water it soon came in :
So, to keep them dry, they wrapped their feet
In a pinky paper, all folded neat ;
    And they fastened it down with a pin.

And they passed the night in a crockery-jar,
And each of them said, " How wise we are !
Though the sky be dark, and the voyage be long,
Yet we never can think we were rash or wrong,
 While round in our sieve we spin."
  Far and few, far and few,
   Are the lands where the Jumblies live :
   Their heads are green, and their hands are blue ;
   And they went to sea in a sieve.

IV.

And all night long they sailed away ;
 And, when the sun went down,
They whistled and warbled a moony song
To the echoing sound of a coppery gong,
 In the shade of the mountains brown.
" O Timballoo !   How happy we are,
When we live in a sieve and a crockery-jar !
And all night long, in the moonlight pale,
We sail away, with a pea-green sail,
 In the shade of the mountains brown.'
  Far and few, far and few,
   Are the lands where the Jumblies live :
   Their heads are green, and their hands are blue ;
   And they went to sea in a sieve.

V.

They sailed to the Western Sea, they did, —
 To a land all covered with trees :
And they bought an owl, and a useful cart,
And a pound of rice, and a cranberry tart,
 And a hive of silvery bees ;

And they bought a pig, and some green jackdaws,
And a lovely monkey with lollipop paws,
And forty bottles of ring-bo-ree,
   And no end of Stilton cheese.
     Far and few, far and few,
       Are the lands where the Jumblies live :
      Their heads are green, and their hands are blue ;
       And they went to sea in a sieve.

VI.

And in twenty years they all came back, —
   In twenty years or more ;
And every one said, " How tall they've grown !
For they've been to the Lakes and the Torrible Zone,
   And the hills of the Chankly Bore."
And they drank their health, and gave them a feast
Of dumplings made of beautiful yeast ;
And every one said, " If we only live,
We, too, will go to sea in a sieve,
   To the hills of the Chankly Bore."
     Far and few, far and few,
       Are the lands where the Jumblies live :
      Their heads are green, and their hands are blue ;
       And they went to sea in a sieve.

                EDWARD LEAR.

6

OLD IRONSIDES

A Y, tear her tattered ensign down !
 Long has it waved on high,
And many an eye has danced to see
 That banner in the sky ;
Beneath it rung the battle shout,
 And burst the cannon's roar ; —
The meteor of the ocean air
 Shall sweep the clouds no more !

Her deck, once red with heroes' blood,
 Where knelt the vanquished foe,
When winds were hurrying o'er the flood,
 And waves were white below,
No more shall feel the victor's tread
 Or know the conquered knee ; —
The harpies of the shore shall pluck
 The eagle of the sea !

Oh, better that her shattered hulk
 Should sink beneath the wave ;
Her thunders shook the mighty deep,
 And there should be her grave ;
Nail to the mast her holy flag,
 Set every threadbare sail,
And give her to the god of storms,
 The lightning and the gale !

OLIVER WENDELL HOLMES.

THE CUMBERLAND.

AT anchor in Hampton Roads we lay,
   On board the Cumberland, sloop-of-war ;
And at times from the fortress across the bay
      The alarum of drums swept past,
      Or a bugle blast
   From the camp on the shore.

Then far away to the south uprose
   A little feather of snow-white smoke,
And we knew that the iron ship of our foes
      Was steadily steering its course
      To try the force
   Of our ribs of oak.

Down upon us heavily runs,
   Silent and sullen, the floating fort ;
Then comes a puff of smoke from her guns,
      And leaps the terrible death,
      With fiery breath,
   From each open port.

We are not idle, but send her straight
   Defiance back in a full broadside !
As hail rebounds from a roof of slate,
      Rebounds our heavier hail
      From each iron scale   ·
   Of the monster's hide.

" Strike your flag ! " the rebel cries,
 In his arrogant old plantation strain.
" Never ! " our gallant Morris replies :
  " It is better to sink than to yield ! "
  And the whole air pealed
 With the cheers of our men.

Then, like a kraken huge and black,
 She crushed our ribs in her iron grasp !
Down went the Cumberland, all a wrack,
  With a sudden shudder of death,
  And the cannon's breath
 For her dying gasp.

Next morn, as the sun rose over the bay,
 Still floated our flag at the mainmast head.
Lord, how beautiful was Thy day !
  Every waft of the air
  Was a whisper of prayer,
 Or a dirge for the dead.

Ho ! brave hearts that went down in the seas !
 Ye are at peace in the troubled stream ;
Ho ! brave land ! with hearts like these,
  Thy flag, that is rent in twain,
  Shall be one again,
 And without a seam !

     HENRY WADSWORTH LONGFELLOW.

YE MARINERS OF ENGLAND.

A Naval Ode.

I.

YE mariners of England,
  That guard our native seas,
Whose flag has braved, a thousand years,
The battle and the breeze,
Your glorious standard launch again
To match another foe!
And sweep through the deep
While the stormy tempests blow;
While the battle rages loud and long,
And the stormy tempests blow.

II.

The spirits of your fathers
Shall start from every wave! —
For the deck it was their field of fame,
And Ocean was their grave:
Where Blake and mighty Nelson fell,
Your manly hearts shall glow,
As ye sweep through the deep,
While the stormy tempests blow;
While the battle rages loud and long,
And the stormy tempests blow.

III.

Britannia needs no bulwark,
No towers along the steep;
Her march is o'er the mountain-waves,
Her home is on the deep.

With thunders from her native oak,
She quells the floods below,
As they roar on the shore,
When the stormy tempests blow ;
When the battle rages loud and long,
And the stormy tempests blow.

IV.

The meteor flag of England
Shall yet terrific burn ;
Till danger's troubled night depart,
And the star of peace return.
Then, then, ye ocean-warriors,
Our song and feast shall flow,
To the fame of your name,
When the storm has ceased to blow ;
When the fiery fight is heard no more,
And the storm has ceased to blow.

THOMAS CAMPBELL.

LOSS OF THE "ROYAL GEORGE."

TOLL for the brave !
The brave that are no more !
All sunk beneath the wave,
Fast by their native shore !

Eight hundred of the brave,
Whose courage well was tried,
Had made the vessel keel,
And laid her on her side.

A land-breeze shook the shrouds,
And she was overset ;
Down went the " Royal George,"
With all her crew complete.

Toll for the brave !
Brave Kempenfelt is gone ;
His last sea-fight is fought,
His work of glory done.

It was not in the battle ;
No tempest gave the shock ;
She sprang no fatal leak,
She ran upon no rock.

His sword was in its sheath,
His fingers held the pen,
When Kempenfelt went down,
With twice four hundred men.

Weigh the vessel up,
Once dreaded by our foes !
And mingle with our cup
The tear that England owes.

Her timbers yet are sound,
And she may float again, —
Full charged with England's thunder,
And plough the distant main :

But Kempenfelt is gone,
His victories are o'er ;
And he and his eight hundred
Shall plough the wave no more.

THE CHAMBERED NAUTILUS.

THIS is the ship of pearl which, poets feign,
        Sails the unshadowed main, —
        The venturous bark that flings
On the sweet summer wind its purpled wings,
In gulfs enchanted where the siren sings,
        And coral reefs lie bare,
Where the cold sea-maids rise to sun their streaming
        hair.

Its webs of living gauze no more unfurl, —
        Wrecked is the ship of pearl!
        And every chambered cell,
Where its dim dreaming life was wont to dwell,
As the frail tenant shaped his growing shell,
        Before thee lies revealed, —
Its irised ceiling rent, its sunless crypt unsealed.

Year after year beheld the silent toil
        That spread his lustrous coil;
        Still, as the spiral grew,
He left the past year's dwelling for the new,
Stole with soft step its shining archway through,
        Built up its idle door,
Stretched in his last-found home, and knew the old no
        more.

Thanks for the heavenly message brought by thee,
        Child of the wandering sea!
        Cast from her lap forlorn,

From thy dead lips a clearer note is born
Than ever Triton blew from wreathèd horn.
　　While on mine ear it rings,
Through the deep caves of thought I hear a voice that
　　　sings : —

Build thee more stately mansions, O my soul,
　　As the swift seasons roll !
　　Leave thy low-vaulted past !
Let each new temple, nobler than the last,
Shut thee from heaven with a dome more vast,
　　Till thou at length art free,
Leaving thine outgrown shell by life's unresting sea !

OLIVER WENDELL HOLMES.

A SEA-SHELL.

SEE what a lovely shell,
　　Small and pure as a pearl,
Lying close to my foot.
　　Frail, but a work divine,
Made so fairily well
　　With delicate spire and whorl.
How exquisitely minute
　　A miracle of design !

The tiny cell is forlorn,
　　Void of the little living will
That made it stir on the shore.
　　Did he stand at the diamond door

Of his house in a rainbow frill ?
  Did he push, when he was uncurled,
A golden foot or a fairy horn
  Through his dim water-world ?

Slight, to be crushed with a tap
  Of my finger-nail on the sand;
Small, but a work divine ;
  Frail, but of force to withstand,
Year upon year, the shock
  Of cataract seas that snap
The three-decker's oaken spine,
  Athwart the ledges of rock,
Here on the Breton strand.

                              ALFRED TENNYSON.

A FISHING-TOWN.

QUAINT clusters of gray houses crowding down
    Unto a river's edge ; the river wide,
And flecked with fishing-boats beyond the town,
Incoming with the slow incoming tide.
Moored to the old pier-end, a smack or two
Slow dandled by the shoreward-setting swell,
And with their nets with every dip wet through,
Show their black, pitchy ribs.   Some far ship's bell
Comes in the capful of light wind that hails

From seaward ; while still louder and more loud,
Beneath the lowering hood of ashen cloud,
Rings the hoarse fisher's shout.   There nearing sails
Loom large and shadowy ; and the sunset gun
Tells that another day is o'er and done.

ANON.

THE BELLS OF LYNN.

O CURFEW of the setting sun ! O bells of Lynn !
  O requiem of the dying day ! O bells of Lynn !

From the dark belfries of yon cloud-cathedral wafted,
Your sounds aerial seem to float, O bells of Lynn !

Borne on the evening wind across the crimson twilight,
O'er land and sea they rise and fall, O bells of Lynn !

The fisherman in his boat, far out beyond the headland,
Listens and leisurely rows ashore, O bells of Lynn !

Over the shining sands, the wandering cattle homeward
Follow each other at your call, O bells of Lynn !

The distant lighthouse hears, and with his flaming
signal
Answers you, passing the watchword on, O bells of
Lynn !

And down the darkening coast run the tumultuous
surges,
And clap their hands and shout to you, O bells of
Lynn !

Till from the shuddering sea, with your wild incan-
  tations,
Ye summon up the spectral moon, O bells of Lynn !

And startled at the sight, like the weird woman of
  Endor,
Ye cry aloud and then are still, O bells of Lynn !

HENRY WADSWORTH LONGFELLOW.

COMING HOME.

THE lift is high and blue,
    And the new moon glints through
The bonnie corn-stooks o' Strathairly ;
    My ship's in Largo Bay,
    And I ken it weel, — the way
Up the steep, steep brae of Strathairly.

    When I sail'd ower the sea, —
    A laddie bold and free, —
The corn sprang green on Strathairly ;
    When I come back again,
    'Tis an auld man walks his lane,
Slow and sad through the fields o' Strathairly.

    Of the shearers that I see,
    Ne'er a body kens me,
Though I kent them a' at Strathairly ;
    And this fisher-wife I pass,
    Can she be the braw lass
That I kiss'd at the back of Strathairly ?

Oh, the land's fine, fine!
I could buy it a' for mine,
My gowd's yellow as the stooks o' Strathairly;
But I fain yon lad wad be,
That sail'd ower the salt sea,
As the dawn rose gray on Strathairly.

D. M. MULOCK.

POMPEII.

THE silence there was what most haunted me.
    Long, speechless streets, whose stepping-stones
        invite
Feet which shall never come; to left and right
Gay colonnades and courts, — beyond the glee,
Heartless, of that forgetful Pagan sea;
On roofless homes and waiting streets, the light
Lies with a pathos sorrowfuller than night.
Fancy forbids this doom of Life with Death
Wedded, and with her wand restores the Life.
The jostling throngs swarm, animate, beneath
The open shops, and all the tropic strife
Of voices, Roman, Greek, Barbarian, mix. The wreath
Indolent hangs on far Vesuvius' crest;
And over all the glowing town and guiltless sea, sweet
    rest.

THOMAS G. APPLETON.

AT DIEPPE.

THE shivering column of the moonlight lies
    Upon the crumbling sea ;
Down the lone shore the flying curlew cries
    Half humanly.

With hoarse, dull wash the backward dragging surge
    Its raucid pebbles rakes,
Or swelling dark runs down with toppling verge,
    And flashing breaks.

The lighthouse flares and darkens from the cliff,
    And stares with lurid eye
Fiercely along the sea and shore, as if
    Some foe to spy.

What knowing thought, O ever-moaning sea,
    Haunts thy perturbed breast, —
What dark crime weighs upon thy memory
    And spoils thy rest?

Thy soft swell lifts and swings the new-launched yacht
    With polished spars and deck,
But crawls and grovels where the bare ribs rot
    Of the old wreck.

O treacherous courtier! thy deceitful lie
    To youth is gayly told,
But in remorse I see thee cringingly
    Crouch to the old.

                              W. W. STORY.

THE PELICAN ISLAND.

L IGHT as a flake of foam upon the wind,
　　Keel-upward from the deep emerged a shell,
Shaped like the moon ere half her horn is filled ;
Fraught with young life, it righted as it rose,
And moved at will along the yielding water.
The native pilot of this little bark
Put out a tier of oars on either side,
Spread to the wafting breeze a twofold sail,
And mounted up and glided down the billow
In happy freedom, pleased to feel the air,
And wander in the luxury of light.
Worth all the dead creation, in that hour,
To me appeared this lonely Nautilus,
My fellow-being, like myself, *alive*.
Entranced in contemplation, vague yet sweet,
I watched its vagrant course and rippling wake,
Till I forgot the sun amidst the heavens.
　It closed, sunk, dwindled to a point, then nothing ;
While the last bubble crowned the dimpling eddy,
Through which my eyes still giddily pursued it,
A joyous creature vaulted through the air, —
The aspiring fish that fain would be a bird,
On long, light wings, that flung a diamond shower
Of dew-drops round its evanescent form,
Sprang into light, and instantly descended.
Ere I could greet the stranger as a friend,
Or mourn his quick departure on the surge,
A shoal of dolphins, tumbling in wild glee,

Glowed with such orient tints they might have been
The rainbow's offspring, when it met the ocean
In that resplendent vision I had seen.
While yet in ecstasy I hung o'er these,
With every motion pouring out fresh beauties,
As though the conscious colors came and went
At pleasure, glorying in their subtle changes, —
Enormous o'er the flood, Leviathan
Looked forth, and from his roaring nostrils sent
Two fountains to the sky, then plunged amain
In headlong pastime through the closing gulf.

JAMES MONTGOMERY.

SANTA CRUZ.

1869.

SAUNTERING hither on listless wings,
    Careless vagabond of the sea,
Little thou heedest the surf that sings,
The bar that thunders, the shale that rings, —
    Give me to keep thy company.

Little thou hast, old friend, that's new,
    Storms and wrecks are old things to thee;
Sick am I of these changes too ;
Little to care for, little to rue, —
    I on the shore, and thou on the sea.

All of thy wanderings far and near
    Bring thee at last to shore and me ;
All of my journeyings end them here,

This our tether must be our cheer, —
    I on the shore, and thou on the sea.

Lazily rocking on ocean's breast,
    Something in common, old friend, have we :
Thou on the shingle seekest thy nest,
I to the waters look for rest, —
    I on the shore, and thou on the sea.

BRET HARTE.

A SEA-VIEW.

I CLIMBED the sea-worn cliffs that edged the shore,
    And looking downward watched the breakers curl
Around the rocks, and marked their mighty swirl
Quiver through swaying seaweed dark and hoar.
Eastward the white caps rose with far-off roar,
Against a sky like red and purple pearl,
Then hollowed greenly in, and rushed to hurl
Their weight of water at the cliffs before.
Only a sea-gull flying silently,
And one soft, rosy sail, were now in sight, —
A sail the sunset touched right tenderly,
And flushed with dreamy glory faintly bright.
Then fain would I have crossed the tossing sea,
Fain dared the storm to float within that light.

ALICE OSBORNE.

HOME-THOUGHTS FROM THE SEA.

NOBLY, nobly Cape Saint Vincent to the north-west
    died away;
Sunset ran, one glorious blood-red, reeking into Cadiz
    Bay;
Bluish 'mid the burning water, full in face Trafalgar
    lay;
In the dimmest north-east distance dawned Gibraltar
    grand and gray;
"Here and here did England help me, — how can I
    help England?" say
Whoso turns as I, this evening, turn to God to praise
    and pray,
While Jove's planet rises yonder, silent, over Africa.

ROBERT BROWNING.

A PICTURE FROM APPLEDORE.

EASTWARD as far as the eye can see,
    Still eastward, eastward endlessly,
The sparkle and tremor of purple sea
That rises before you, a flickering hill,
On and on to the shut of the sky;
And, beyond, you fancy it sloping until
The same multitudinous throb and thrill
That vibrate under your dizzy eye,

In ripples of orange and pink, are sent
Where the poppied sails doze on the yard,
And the clumsy junk and proa lie,
Sunk deep with precious woods and nard,
'Mid the palmy isles of the Orient.
Those leaning towers of clouded white,
On the farthest brink of doubtful ocean,
That shorten and shorten out of sight,
Yet seem on the self-same spot to stay,
Receding with a motionless motion,
Fading to dubious films of gray,
Lost, dimly found, then vanished wholly,
Will rise again, the great world under,
First films, then towers, then high-heaped
    clouds,
Whose nearing outlines sharpen slowly
Into tall ships with cobweb shrouds,
That fill long Mongol eyes with wonder,
Crushing the violet wave to spray,
Past some low headland of Cathay : —
What was that sigh that seemed so near,
Chilling your fancy to the core ?
'Tis only the sad old sea you hear,
That seems to seek for evermore
Something it cannot find, and so,
Sighing, seeks on, and tells its woe
To the pitiless breakers of Appledore.

JAMES R. LOWELL.

DOVER BEACH.

THE sea is calm to-night,
The tide is full, the moon lies fair
Upon the Straits ; on the French coast the light
Gleams and is gone ; the cliffs of England stand
Glimmering and vast out in the tranquil bay.
Come to the window, sweet is the night air !
Only from the long line of spray,
Where the ebb meets the moon-blanched sand,
Listen ! you hear the grating roar
Of pebbles, which the waves suck back and fling,
At their return, up the high strand,
Begin and cease, and then again begin,
With tremulous cadence slow, and bring
The eternal note of sadness in.

Sophocles long ago
Heard it on the Ægean, and it brought
Into his mind the turbid ebb and flow
Of human misery : we
Find also in the sound a thought,
Hearing it by this distant northern sea.
The sea of faith
Was once too at the full, and round earth's shore
Lay like the folds of a bright girdle furled ;
But now I only hear
Its melancholy, long withdrawing roar,
Retreating to the breath
Of the night wind down the vast edges drear
And naked shingles of the world.

Ah, love, let us be true
To one another ! for the world which seems
To lie before us like a land of dreams,
    So various, so beautiful, so new,
Hath really neither joy, nor love, nor light,
Nor certitude, nor peace, nor help for pain ;
And we are here as on a darkling plain,
Swept with confused alarms of struggle and fight,
    Where ignorant armies clash by night.

MATTHEW ARNOLD.

AT BAY RIDGE, L.I.

PLEASANT it is to lie amid the grass
    Under these shady locusts half the day,
Watching the ships reflected in the Bay,
    Topmast and shroud, as in a wizard's glass ;
To see the happy-hearted martins pass,
    Brushing the dew-drops from the lilac spray ;
Or else to hang enamoured o'er some lay
    Of fairy regions, or to muse, alas !
On Dante exiled journeying outworn ;
    On patient Milton's sorrowfullest eyes,
Shut from the splendors of the Night and Morn ;
    To think that now beneath the Italian skies,
In such clear air as this, by Tiber's wave
    Daisies are trembling over Keats's grave.

THOMAS BAILEY ALDRICH.

AT CARNAC.

May 6, 1859.

FAR on its rocky knoll descried,
    Saint Michael's chapel cuts the sky.
I climbed ; beneath me bright and wide
    Lay the lone coast of Brittany.

Bright in the sunset, weird and still,
    It lay beside the Atlantic wave,
As if the wizard Merlin's will
    Yet charmed it from his forest grave.

Beside me, on their grassy sweep,
    Bearded with lichen scrawled and gray,
The giant stones of Carnac sleep,
    In the mild evening of the May.

No priestly, stern procession now
    Streams through the rows of pillars old ;
No victims bleed, no Druids bow ;
    Sheep make the furze-grown aisles their fold.

From bush to bush the cuckoo flies,
    The orchis red gleams everywhere ;
Gold broom with furze in blossom vies,
    The blue-bells perfume all the air.

And o'er the glistening, lonely land,
    Rise up all round the Christian spires ;
The church of Carnac by the strand
    Catches the westering sun's last fires.

And there, across the watery way,
  See, low above the tide at flood,
The sickle-sweep of Quiberon Bay,
  Whose beach once ran with royal blood.

And, beyond that, the Atlantic wide !
  All round no soul, no boat, no hail !
But, on the horizon's verge descried,
  Hangs, touched with light, one snowy sail !

MATTHEW ARNOLD.

THE SAND-PIPER.

ACROSS the narrow beach we flit,
  One little sand-piper and I,
And fast I gather, bit by bit,
  The scattered driftwood bleached and dry.
The wild waves reach their hands for it,
  The wild wind raves, the tide runs high,
As up and down the beach we flit, —
  One little sand-piper and I.

Above our heads the sullen clouds
  Scud black and swift across the sky;
Like silent ghosts in misty shrouds
  Stand out the white lighthouses high.
Almost as far as eye can reach,
  I see the close-reefed vessels fly,
As fast we flit along the beach, —
  One little sand-piper and I.

I watch him as he skims along,
　Uttering his sweet and mournful cry.
He starts not at my fitful song,
　Or flash of fluttering drapery.
He has no thought of any wrong ;
　He scans me with a fearless eye.
Stanch friends are we, well tried and strong,
　The little sand-piper and I.

Comrade, where wilt thou be to-night,
　When the loosed storm breaks furiously ?
My driftwood fire will burn so bright !
　To what warm shelter canst thou fly ?
I do not fear for thee, though wroth
　The tempest rushes through the sky :
For are we not God's children both,
　Thou, little sand-piper, and I ?

CELIA THAXTRR.

THE STORMY PETREL.

A THOUSAND miles from land are we,
　　Tossing about on the stormy sea,
From billow to bounding billow cast,
Like fleecy snow on the stormy blast.
The sails are scattered abroad like weeds ;
The strong masts shake like quivering reeds ;
The mighty cables and iron chains,
The hull, which all earthly strength disdains, —
They strain and they crack ; and hearts like stone
Their natural, hard, proud strength disown.

Up and down ! up and down !
From the base of the wave to the billow's crown,
And amidst the flashing and feathery foam,
The stormy petrel finds a home.
A home ! if such a place may be
For her who lives on the wide, wide sea,
On the craggy ice, in the frozen air,
And only seeketh her rocky lair
To warm her young, and to teach them to spring
At once o'er the waves on their stormy wing.

O'er the deep ! o'er the deep !
Where the whale and the shark and the sword-fish
    sleep,
Outflying the blast and the driving rain,
The petrel telleth her tale — in vain ;
For the mariner curseth the warning bird
Which bringeth him news of the storm unheard !
Ah ! thus does the prophet of good or ill
Meet hate from the creatures he serveth still ;
Yet he ne'er falters, — so, petrel, spring
Once more o'er the waves on thy stormy wing !

BARRY CORNWALL.

THE OCEAN.

THERE is a pleasure in the pathless woods,
    There is a rapture on the lonely shore,
There is society, where none intrudes,
    By the deep sea, and music in its roar ;

I love not Man the less, but Nature more,
From these our interviews, in which I steal
From all I may be, or have been before,
To mingle with the Universe, and feel
What I can ne'er express, yet cannot all conceal.

Roll on, thou deep and dark blue ocean, —roll!
Ten thousand fleets sweep over thee in vain ;
Man marks the earth with ruin, —his control
Stops with the shore ; upon the watery plain
The wrecks are all thy deed, nor doth remain
A shadow of man's ravage, save his own,
When, for a moment, like a drop of rain,
He sinks into thy depths with bubbling groan,
Without a grave, unknelled, uncoffined, and unknown.

His steps are not upon thy paths, — thy fields
Are not a spoil for him, — thou dost arise
And shake him from thee ; the vile strength he wields
For earth's destruction, thou dost all despise,
Spurning him from thy bosom to the skies,
And send'st him, shivering, in thy playful spray,
And howling, to his gods, where haply lies
His petty hope in some near port or bay,
And dashest him again to earth : there let him lay.

The armaments which thunder-strike the walls
Of rock-built cities, bidding nations quake,
And monarchs tremble in their capitals ;
The oak leviathans, whose huge ribs make

Their clay creator the vain title take
Of lord of thee, and arbiter of war;
These are thy toys, and as the snowy flake
They melt into thy yeast of waves, which mar
Alike the Armada's pride, or spoils of Trafalgar.

Thy shores are empires, changed in all save thee, —
Assyria, Greece, Rome, Carthage, what are they?
Thy waters wasted them while they were free,
And many a tyrant since; their shores obey
The stranger, slave, or savage; their decay
Has dried up realms to deserts: not so thou,
Unchangeable save to thy wild waves' play, —
Time writes no wrinkles on thy azure brow, —
Such as creation's dawn beheld, thou rollest now.

Thou glorious mirror, where th' Almighty's form
Glasses itself in tempests; in all time,
Calm or convulsed, — in breeze, or gale, or storm,
Icing the pole, or in the torrid clime
Dark-heaving; boundless, endless, and sublime, —
The image of eternity, — the throne
Of th' Invisible; even from out thy slime
The monsters of the deep are made; each zone
Obeys thee; thou goest forth, dread, fathomless, alone.

And I have loved thee, Ocean! and my joy
Of youthful sports was on thy breast to be
Borne, like thy bubbles, onward; from a boy
I wantoned with thy breakers, — they to me

Were a delight ; and if the fresh'ning sea
Made them a terror, 'twas a pleasing fear,
For I was, as it were, a child of thee,
And trusted to thy billows far and near,
And laid my hand upon thy mane — as I do here.

BYRON.

TEMPTATION.

THE billows swell, the winds are high,
    Clouds overcast my wintry sky ;
Out of the depths to Thee I call, —
My fears are great, my strength is small.

O Lord, the pilot's part perform,
And guard and guide me through the storm,
Defend me from each threatening ill,
Control the waves, say, " Peace, be still ! "

Amidst the roaring of the sea,
My soul still hangs her hope on Thee ;
Thy constant love, thy faithful care,
Is all that saves me from despair.

Dangers of every shape and name
Attend the followers of the Lamb,
Who leave the world's deceitful shore,
And leave it to return no more.

Though tempest-toss'd and half a wreck,
My Saviour through the floods I seek;
Let neither winds nor stormy main
Force back my shatter'd bark again.

WILLIAM COWPER.

QUA CURSUM VENTUS.

AS ships, becalmed at eve, that lay,
 With canvas drooping, side by side,
Two towers of sail, at dawn of day,
 Are scarce, long leagues apart, descried :

When fell the night, upsprung the breeze,
 And all the darkling hours they plied ;
Nor dreamt but each the self-same seas
 By each was cleaving, side by side ;

E'en so —- but why the tale reveal
 Of those whom, year by year unchanged,
Brief absence joined anew, to feel,
 Astounded, soul from soul estranged.

At dead of night their sails were filled,
 And onward each rejoicing steered ;
Ah, neither blame, for neither willed
 Or wist what first with dawn appeared.

To veer, how vain ! On, onward strain,
 Brave barks ! In light, in darkness too !
Through winds and tides one compass guides, —
 To that and your own selves be true.

But O blithe breeze ! and O great seas !
  Though ne'er, that earliest parting past,
On your wide plain they join again,
  Together lead them home at last.

One port, methought, alike they sought, —
  One purpose hold, where'er they fare ;
O bounding breeze, O rushing seas,
  At last, at last, unite them there !

ARTHUR HUGH CLOUGH.

THE PILGRIMS.

UPON the white sea-sand
    There sat a pilgrim-band,
Telling the losses that their lives had known,
    While evening waned away
    From breezy cliff and bay,
And the strong tides went out with weary moan.

    One spake, with quivering lip,
    Of a fair-freighted ship,
With all his household, to the deep gone down ;
    And one had wilder woe,
    For a fair face long ago
Lost in the darker depths of a great town.

    There were who mourned their youth
    With a most loving truth,
For its brave hopes and memories ever green ;
    And one upon the west
    Turned an eye that would not rest,
For far-off hills whereon his joy had been.

Some talked of vanished gold,
Some of proud honors told,
Some spake of friends that were their trust no more;
And one of a green grave,
Beside a foreign wave,
That made him sit so lonely on the shore.

But when their tales were done,
There spake among them one, —
A stranger, seeming from all sorrow free, —
" Sad losses have ye met,
But mine is heavier yet,
For a believing heart hath gone from me."

" Alas ! " these pilgrims said,
" For the living and the dead,
For fortune's cruelty and love's sure cross,
For the wrecks of land and sea !
But, however it came to thee,
Thine, stranger, is life's last and heaviest loss ! "

FRANCES BROWN.

"SPOKEN."

COUNTING the hours by bells and lights,
    We rose and sank ;
The waves, on royal banquet-heights,
    Tossed off and drank
Their jewels made of sun and moon,
White pearls at midnight, gold at noon.

Counting the hours by bells and lights,
  We sailed and sailed ;
Six lonely days, six lonely nights,
  No ship we hailed.
Till all the sea seemed bound in spell,
And silence sounded like a knell.

At last, just when by bells and lights
  Of seventh day
The dawn grew clear, in sudden flights
  White sails away
To east, like birds, went spreading slow
Their wings, which reddened in the glow.

No more we count the bells and lights :
  We laugh for joy !
The trumpets with their brazen mights
  Call, " Ship ahoy ! "
We hold each other's hands ; our cheeks
Are wet with tears ; but no one speaks.

In instant comes the sun, and lights
  The ship with fire ;
Each mast creeps up to dizzy heights,
  A blazing spire ;
One faint " Ahoy," then all in vain
We look ; we are alone again.

I have forgotten bells and lights,
  And waves which drank
Their jewels up ; those days and nights,
  Which rose and sank,

Have turned like other pasts, and fled,
And carried with them all their dead.

But every day that fire-ship lights
  My distant blue,
And every day glad wonder smites
  My heart anew,
How in that instant each could heed,
And hear the other's swift " God-speed ! "

Counting by hours thy days and nights
  In weariness,
O patient soul, on godlike heights
  Of loneliness,
I passed thee by ; tears filled our eyes ;
The loud winds mocked and drowned our cries.

The hours go by, with bells and lights ;
  We sail, we drift ;
Our souls, in changing tasks and rites,
  Find work and shrift.
But this I pray, and praying know,
Till faith almost to joy can grow,

That hour by hour the bells, the lights,
  Of sound, of flame,
Weave spell which ceaselessly recites
  To thee a name,
And smiles which thou canst not forget
For thee are suns which never set.

       H. H.

8

SEEN AND UNSEEN.

THE wind ahead, the billows high,
 A whited wave, but sable sky,
And many a league of tossing sea
Between the hearts I love and me. ·

The wind ahead: day after day
These weary words the sailors say;
To weeks the days are lengthened now,—
Still mounts the surge to meet our prow.

Through longing day and lingering night
I still accuse Time's lagging flight,
Or gaze out o'er the envious sea,
That keeps the hearts I love from me.

Yet, ah, how shallow is all grief!
How instant is the deep relief!
And what a hypocrite am I
To feign forlorn, to 'plain and sigh!

The wind ahead? The wind is free!
Forevermore it favoreth me,
To shores of God still blowing fair,
O'er seas of God my bark doth bear.

This surging brine *I* do not sail,
This blast adverse is not my gale;
'Tis here I only seem to be,
But really sail another sea, —

Another sea, pure sky its waves,
Whose beauty hides no heaving graves, —
A sea all haven, whereupon
No hapless bark to wreck has gone.

The winds that o'er my ocean run
Reach through all heavens beyond the sun ;
Through life and death, through fate, through time,
Grand breaths of God, they sweep sublime.

Eternal trades, they cannot veer,
And, blowing, teach us how to steer ;
And well for him whose joy, whose care,
Is but to keep before them fair.

Oh, thou God's mariner, heart of mine,
Spread canvas to the airs divine !
Spread sail ! and let thy Fortune be
Forgotten in thy Destiny.

For Destiny pursues us well,
By sea, by land, through heaven or hell :
It suffers Death alone to die,
Bids Life all change and chance defy.

Would earth's dark ocean suck thee down ?
Earth's ocean thou, O Life, shalt drown,
Shalt flood it with thy finer wave,
And, sepulchred, entomb thy grave !

Life loveth life and good ; then trust
What most the spirit would, it must ;
Deep wishes, in the heart that be,
Are blossoms of Necessity.

A thread of Law runs through thy prayer,
Stronger than iron cables are ;
And Love and Longing toward her goal
Are pilots sweet to guide the Soul.

So Life must live, and Soul must sail,
And Unseen over Seen prevail,
And all God's argosies come to shore,
Let ocean smile, or rage and roar.

And so, 'mid storm or calm, my bark
With snowy wake still nears her mark ;
Cheerly the trades of being blow,
And sweeping down the wind I go.

D. A. WASSON.

AT SEA.

THE night is made for cooling shade,
　For silence and for sleep ;
And when I was a child, I laid
My hands upon my breast and prayed,
　And sank to slumbers deep :
Child-like as then I lie to-night,
And watch my lonely cabin light.

Each movement of the swaying lamp
　Shows how the vessel reels,
As o'er her deck the billows tramp,
And all her timbers strain and cramp,
　With every shock she feels.
It starts and shudders, while it burns,
And in its hingèd socket turns.

Now swinging slow, and slanting low,
    It almost level lies ;
And yet I know, while to and fro
I watch the seeming pendule go
    With restless fall and rise,
The steady shaft is still upright,
Poising its little globe of light.

O hand of God ! O lamp of peace !
    O promise of my soul !
Though weak, and tossed, and ill at ease,
Amid the roar of smiting seas,
    The ship's convulsive roll,
I own, with love and tender awe,
Yon perfect type of perfect law !

A heavenly trust my spirit calms,
    My soul is filled with light :
The ocean sings his solemn psalms,
The wild winds chant : I cross my palms,
    Happy as if, to-night,
Under the cottage roof, again
I heard the soothing summer rain.

J. T. Trowbridge.

A NAME IN THE SAND.

ALONE I walked the ocean strand ;
    A pearly shell was in my hand :
I stooped and wrote upon the sand
    My name, the year, the day.

As onward from the spot I passed,
One lingering look behind I cast:
A wave came rolling high and fast,
  And washed my lines away.

And so, methought, 'twill shortly be
With every mark on earth from me :
A wave of dark Oblivion's sea
  Will sweep across the place
Where I have trod the sandy shore
Of Time, and been to be no more, —
Of me, my day, the name I bore,
  To leave nor track nor trace.

And yet, with Him who counts the sands,
And holds the waters in his hands,
I know a lasting record stands,
  Inscribed against my name,
Of all this mortal part has wrought,
Of all this thinking soul has thought,
And from these fleeting moments caught
  For glory or for shame.

HANNAH F. GOULD.

SEA-SHORE.

I HEARD, or seemed to hear, the chiding Sea
  Say, Pilgrim, why so late and slow to come?
Am I not always here, thy summer home?
Is not my voice thy music, morn and eve?
My breath, thy healthful climate in the heats,
My touch thy antidote, my bay thy bath?

Was ever building like my terraces ?
Was ever couch magnificent as mine ?
Lie on the warm rock-ledges, and there learn
A little hut suffices like a town.
I make your sculptured architecture vain,
Vain beside mine.   I drive my wedges home,
And carve the coastwise mountain into caves.
Lo ! here is Rome, and Nineveh, and Thebes,
Karnak, and Pyramid, and Giant's Stairs,
Half piled or prostrate ; and my newest slab
Older than all thy race.
                         Behold the Sea,
The opaline, the plentiful and strong,
Yet beautiful as is the rose in June,
Fresh as the trickling rainbow of July ;
Sea full of food, the nourisher of kinds,
Purger of earth, and medicine of men ;
Creating a sweet climate by my breath,
Washing out harms and griefs from memory,
And, in my mathematic ebb and flow,
Giving a hint of that which changes not.
Rich are the sea-gods ; — who gives gifts but they ?
They grope the sea for pearls, but more than pearls :
They pluck Force thence, and give it to the wise.
For every wave is wealth to Dædalus,
Wealth to the cunning artist who can work
This matchless strength.   Where shall he find, O
    waves !
A load your Atlas shoulders cannot lift ?
  I with my hammer, pounding evermore
The rocky coast, smite Andes into dust,

Strewing my bed, and, in another age
Rebuild a continent of better men.
Then I unbar the doors : my paths lead out
The exodus of nations : I disperse
Men to all shores that front the hoary main.

I, too, have arts and sorceries ;
Illusion dwells for ever with the wave.
I know what spells are laid.   Leave me to deal
With credulous and imaginative man ;
For, though he scoop my water in his palm,
A few rods off he deems it gems and clouds.
Planting strange fruits and sunshine on the shore,
I make some coast alluring, some lone isle,
To distant men, who must go there, or die.

RALPH WALDO EMERSON.

MY LIFE IS LIKE A STROLL UPON THE BEACH.

MY life is like a stroll upon the beach,
    As near the ocean's edge as I can go ;
My tardy steps its waves sometimes o'erreach,
    Sometimes I stay to let them overflow.

My sole employment 'tis, and scrupulous care,
    To place my gains beyond the reach of tides ;
Each smoother pebble, and each shell more rare,
    Which ocean kindly to my hand confides.

I have but few companions on the shore,
    They scorn the strand who sail upon the sea ;
Yet oft I think the ocean they've sailed o'er
    Is deeper known upon the strand to me.

The middle sea contains no crimson dulse,
  Its deeper waves cast up no pearls to view;
Along the shore my hand is on its pulse,
  And I converse with many a shipwrecked crew.

HENRY D. THOREAU.

LINES ON NEW HAMPSHIRE MEN GOING TO SEA.

THOUGH all the fates should prove unkind,
    Leave not your native land behind.
The ship, becalmed, at length stands still ;
The steed must rest beneath the hill ;
But swiftly still our fortunes pace,
To find us out in every place.

The vessel, though her masts be firm,
Beneath her copper bears a worm ;
Around the cape, across the line,
Till fields of ice her course confine ;
It matters not how smooth the breeze,
How shallow or how deep the seas,
Whether she bears Manilla twine,
Or in her hold Madeira wine,
Or China teas, or Spanish hides,
In port or quarantine she rides ;
Far from New England's blustering shore,
New England's worm her hulk shall bore,
And sink her in the Indian seas,
Twine, wine, and hides, and China teas.

HENRY D. THOREAU.

CHILDREN ON THE SHORE.

WE are building little homes on the sands,
    We are making little rooms very gay,
We are busy with our hearts and our hands,
    We are sorry that the time flits away.
Oh, why are the minutes in such haste ?
    Oh, why don't they leave us to our play ?
Our lessons and our meals are such waste !
    We can dine very well another day.

We do not mind the tide coming in,
    We can dig it a cunning little bed,
Or leave our pretty house and begin
    Another pretty house in its stead ;
We do not mind the sun in our eyes,
    When it makes such a dazzle of the world
That we cannot tell the sea from the skies,
    Nor look where the flying drops are hurled.

The shells that we gather are so fair,
    The birds and the clouds are so kind,
And the winds are so merry with our hair,
    It is only the *People* that we mind !
Papa, if you come so very near,
    We can't build the library to-day ;
We think you are tired of being here,
    And perhaps you would like to go away.

There are just one or two we won't refuse,
  If they come by, to help us now and then;
But we want only friends to be of use,
  And not all these idle grown men.
Perhaps if we hurry very much,
  And don't lose an instant of the day,
There'll be time for the last lovely touch,
  Before the sea sweeps it all away !

ANON.

DEEP-SEA SOUNDINGS.

MARINER, what of the deep?
                    This of the deep:
Twilight is there, and solemn, changeless calm;
Beauty is there, and tender, healing balm, —
Balm with no root in earth, or air, or sea;
Poised by the finger of God, it floateth free,
And, as it treadeth the waves, the sound doth rise,
Hither shall come no farther sacrifice;
Never again the anguished clutch at life,
Never again great Love and Death at strife.
He who hath suffered all need fear no more,
Quiet his portion now for evermore.

Mariner, what of the deep?
                    This of the deep:
Solitude dwells not there, though silence reign;
Mighty the brotherhood of loss and pain;
There is communion past the need of speech,
There is a love no words of love can reach;

Heavy the waves that superincumbent press,
But as we labor here with constant stress,
Hand doth hold out to hand not help alone,
But the deep bliss of being fully known.
There are no kindred like the kin of sorrow,
There is no hope like theirs who fear no morrow.

Mariner, what of the deep ?
                         This of the deep :
Though we have travelled past the line of day,
Glory of night doth light us on our way ;
Radiance that comes we know not how or whence,
Rainbows without the rain past duller sense,
Music of hidden reefs and waves long past,
Thunderous organ-tones from far-off blast,
Harmony victrix clothed in state sublime,
Couched on the wrecks begemmed with pearls of time ;
Never a wreck but brings some beauty here ;
Down where the waves are stilled, the sea shines
      clear ;
Deeper than life, the plan of life doth lie.
He who knows all fears naught. Great Death shall
      die.

                                        ANON.

FROM "IN MEMORIAM."

FAIR ship that from the Italian shore
      Sailest the placid ocean plains,
      With my lost Arthur's loved remains,
Spread thy full wings and waft him o'er !

So draw him home to those that mourn
    In vain ; a favorable speed
    Ruffle thy mirrored mast, and lead
Through prosperous floods his holy urn !

All night no ruder air perplex
    Thy sliding keel, till Phosphor, bright
    As our pure love, through early light
Shall glimmer on the dewy decks !

Sphere all your lights around, above ;
    Sleep, gentle heavens, before the prow ;
    Sleep, gentle winds, as he sleeps now,
My friend, the brother of my love !

My Arthur, whom I shall not see
    Till all my widowed race be run ;
    Dear as the mother to the son,
More than my brothers are to me !

I hear the noise about thy keel ;
    I hear the bell struck in the night ;
    I see the cabin window bright ;
I see the sailor at the wheel.

Thou bringest the sailor to his wife,
    And travelled men from foreign lands ;
    And letters unto trembling hands ;
And thy dark freight, a vanished life.

So bring him : we have idle dreams ;
    This look of quiet flatters thus
    Our home-bred fancies ; oh, to us,
The fools of habit, sweeter seems

To rest beneath the clover sod,
 That takes the sunshine and the rains,
 Or where the kneeling hamlet drains
The chalice of the grapes of God ;

Than if with thee the roaring wells
 Should gulf him fathom deep in brine,
 And hands so often clasped in mine
Should toss with tangle and with shells.

Thou comest much wept for ; such a breeze
 Compelled thy canvas, and my prayer
 Was as the whisper of an air,
To breathe thee over lonely seas.

For I in spirit saw thee move
 Through circles of the bounding sky,
 Week after week ; the days go by ;
Come quick, thou bringest all I love.

Henceforth, wherever thou mayest roam,
 My blessing, like a line of light,
 Is on the waters day and night,
And, like a beacon, guards thee home.

So may whatever tempest mars
 Mid-ocean spare thee, sacred bark,
 And balmy drops in summer dark
Slide from the bosom of the stars.

So kind an office hath been done,
 Such precious relics brought by thee ;
 The dust of him I shall not see,
Till all my widowed race be run.
ALFRED TENNYSON.

UNDER THE SURFACE.

I.

ON the surface, foam and roar,
    Restless heave and passionate dash ;
Shingle rattle along the shore,
    Gathering boom and thundering crash.

· Under the surface, soft green light,
    A hush of peace and an endless calm,
Wind and waves from a choral height
    Falling sweet as a far-off psalm.

On the surface, swell and swirl,
    Tossing weed and drifting waif,
Broken spars that the mad waves whirl,
    Where round wreck-watching rocks they chafe.

Under the surface, loveliest forms,
    Feathery fronds with crimson curl, —
Treasures too deep for the raid of storms, —
    Delicate coral and hidden pearl.

II.

On the surface, lilies white,
    A painted skiff with a singing crew,
Sky reflections soft and bright,
    Tremulous crimson, gold, and blue.

Under the surface, life in death,
  Slimy tangle and oozy moans,
Creeping things with watery breath,
  Blackening roots and whitening bones.

On the surface, a shining reach,
  A crystal couch for the moonbeam's rest,
Starry ripples along the beach,
  Sunset songs from the breezy west.

Under the surface, glooms and fears,
  Treacherous currents, swift and strong,
Deafening rush in the drowning ears. —
  Have ye rightly read my song?

FRANCES RIDLEY HAVERGALL.

SHIPS AT SEA.

I HAVE ships that went to sea
  More than fifty years ago;
None have yet come home to me,
  But are sailing to and fro.
I have seen them in my sleep,
Plunging through the shoreless deep,
With tattered sails, and battered hulls,
While around them screamed the gulls,
  Flying low, — flying low.

I have wondered why they stayed
  From me, sailing round the world;
And I've said, " I'm half afraid
  That their sails will ne'er be furled."

Great the treasure that they hold, —
Silks, and plumes, and bars of gold;
While the spices that they bear
Fill with fragrance all the air,
    As they sail, — as they sail.

Ah ! each sailor in the port
  Knows that I have ships at sea,
Of the waves and winds the sport ;
  And the sailors pity me.
Oft they come and with me walk,
Cheering me with hopeful talk,
Till I put my fears aside,
And, contented, watch the tide
    Rise and fall, — rise and fall.

I have waited on the piers,
  Gazing for them down the bay,
Days and nights, for many years,
  Till I've turned, heart-sick, away.
But the pilots, when they land,
Stop and take me by the hand,
Saying, " You will like to see
Your proud ships come home from sea,
    One and all, — one and all."

So I never quite despair,
  Nor let hope nor courage fail ;
And some day, when skies are fair,
  Up the bay my ships will sail.

I shall buy then all I need, —
Prints to look at, books to read,
Horses, wines, and works of art,
Everything, — except a heart.
    That is lost, — that is lost !

Once when I was pure and young,
   Richer too than I am now,
Ere a cloud was o'er me flung,
Or a wrinkle crossed my brow,
There was one whose heart was mine ;
But she's something now divine,
And though come my ships from sea,
They can bring no heart to me
    Evermore, — evermore.

BARRY GRAY.

THE TWO SHIPS.

A S I stand by the cross on the lone mountain's
      crest,
   Looking over the ultimate sea,
In the gloom of the mountain a ship lies at rest,
   And one sails away from the lea :
One spreads its white wings on a far-reaching track,
   With pennant and sheet flowing free ;
One hides in the shadow, with sails laid aback, —
   The ship that is waiting for me !

But lo! in the distance the clouds break away!
    The Gate's glowing portal I see;
And I hear from the outgoing ship in the bay
    The song of the sailors in glee:
So I think of the luminous footprints that bore
    The comfort o'er dark Galilee,
And wait for the signal to go to the shore,
    To the ship that is waiting for me.

                        BRET HARTE.

MY SHIP.

DOWN to the wharves, as the sun goes down,
    And the daylight's tumult and dust and din
Are dying away in the busy town,
    I go to see if my ship comes in.

I gaze far over the quiet sea,
    Rosy with sunset, like mellow wine,
Where ships, like lilies, lie tranquilly,
    Many and fair, — but I see not mine.

I question the sailors every night,
    Who over the bulwarks idly lean,
Noting the sails as they come in sight, —
    " Have you seen my beautiful ship come in?"

"Whence does she come?" they ask of me;
    " Who is her master, and what her name?"
And they smile upon me pityingly,
    When my answer is ever and ever the same.

Oh, mine was a vessel of strength and truth,
   Her sails were white as a young lamb's fleece,
She sailed long since from the port of Youth, —
   Her master was Love, and her name was Peace.

And, like all beloved and beauteous things,
   She faded in distance and doubt away, —
With only a tremble of snowy wings
   She floated, swan-like, adown the bay,

Carrying with her a precious freight, —
   All I had gathered by years of pain;
A tempting prize to the pirate, Fate, —
   And still I watch for her back again; —

Watch from the earliest morning light,
   Till the pale stars grieve o'er the dying day,
To catch the gleam of her canvas white
   Among the islands which gem the bay.

But she comes not yet, — she will never come
   To gladden my eyes and my spirit more;
And my heart grows hopeless and faint and dumb,
   As I wait and wait on the lonesome shore,

Knowing that tempest and time and storm
   Have wrecked and shattered my beauteous bark;
Rank sea-weeds cover her wasting form,
   And her sails are tattered and stained and dark.

But the tide comes up, and the tide goes down,
  And the daylight follows the night's eclipse, —
And still with the sailors, tanned and brown,
  I wait on the wharves and watch the ships.

And still with a patience that is not hope,
  For vain and empty it long hath been,
I sit on the rough shore's rocky slope,
  And watch to see if my ship comes in.

ELIZABETH AKERS.

A QUEST.

ALL in the summer even,
    When sea and sky were bright,
As royally the sunset
    Went forth to meet the night,

My Love and I were sailing
    Into the shining west,
To find some Happy Island,
    Some Paradise of rest.

We steered where sunset splendor
    Turned into gold the shore ;
The rocks behind its brightness
    Were cruel as before.

Within the caves sang sirens,
    But there the whirlpools be ;
Not there the Happy Islands,
    Not there the peaceful sea.

Toward the deep mid-ocean
   Tides ran and swift winds blew;
It must be there those Islands
   Await the longing view.

Their shores are soft with verdure,
   Their skies for ever fair,
And always is the fragrance
   Of blossoms on the air.

I set our sail to seek them,
   But she, my Love, drew back:
" Not yet ; the night is chilly,
   I fear that unknown track."

So home we sailed, at twilight,
   To the familiar shore ;
Turned from the golden glory,
   To live the old life o'er.

We'll make no further ventures, —
   For timid is my Love, —
Until fresh sailing orders
   Are sent us from above.

Then to the deep mid-ocean
   Though we reluctant sail,
We'll find our Happy Islands
   And joys that cannot fail.

LOUISE CHANDLER MOULTON.

MY SEAWARD WINDOW.

THE sweet moon rules the east to-night,
　　To show the sun she too can shine, —
From his forsaken cell of night
　　She builds herself a jewelled shrine.

From my lone window look I forth
　　Where the grim headlands point to sea,
And think how out between them passed
　　The ship that bore my friend from me.

A track of silvery splendor leads
　　To where my straining sight was stayed;
It may be there our two souls met,
　　And vows of earnest import made.

But then the autumn noontide glow
　　O'er the still sea stretched far and wide,
While kneeling, watching from the cliff,
　　" My friend is dear to me ! " I cried.

My little children dancing cried,
　　" Why do you kneel and gaze so far ? "
" I kneel to bless my parting friend,
　　And even ye forgotten are."

And one might ask, " What boots this song
　　Sung lonely to yon wintry skies ? "
It leads me by a holier light
　　Where Memory's solemn comfort lies.

JULIA WARD HOWE.

THE SEA.

FOR lo! the sea that fleets about the land,
    And like a girdle clips her solid waist,
Music and measure both doth understand :
    For his great crystal eye is always cast
Up to the moon, and on her fixèd fast ;
And as she danceth in her pallid sphere,
So danceth he about the centre here.

Sometimes his proud green waves, in order set,
    One after other flow into the shore,
Which, when they have with many kisses wet,
    They ebb away in order as before.
And to make known his courtly love the more,
He oft doth lay aside his three-forkt mace,
And with his arms the timorous earth embrace.

JOHN DAVIES, 1596.

BY THE SEA.

IT is a beauteous evening, calm and free ;
    The holy time is quiet as a nun
Breathless with adoration ; the broad sun
Is sinking down in its tranquillity.

The gentleness of heaven is on the sea ;
Listen ! the mighty being is awake,
And doth with his eternal motion make
A sound like thunder — everlastingly.

Dear child! dear girl! that walkest with me here,
If thou appear untouched by solemn thought,
Thy nature is not therefore less divine :

Thou liest in Abraham's bosom all the year,
And worship'st at the Temple's inner shrine,
God being with thee when we know it not.

WILLIAM WORDSWORTH.

THE MARINERS.

RAISE we the yard and ply the oar,
   The breeze is calling us swift away;
The waters are breaking in foam on the shore ;
   Our boat no more can stay, can stay.

When the blast flies fast in the clouds on high,
   And billows are roaring loud below,
The boatman's song, in the stormy sky,
   Still dares the gale to blow, to blow.

The timber that frames his faithful boat
   Was dandled in storms on the mountain peaks,
And in storms, with a bounding keel, 'twill float,
   And laugh when the sea-fiend shrieks, and shrieks.

And then, in the calm and glistening nights,
   We have tales of wonder, and joy, and fear,
And deeds of the powerful ocean sprites,
   With which our hearts we cheer, we cheer.

For often the dauntless mariner knows
   That he must sink to the land beneath,
Where the diamond on trees of coral grows,
   In the emerald halls of Death, of Death.

Onward we sweep through smooth and storm ;
   We are voyagers all in shine or gloom ;
And the dreamer who skulks by his chimney warm
   Drifts in his sleep to doom, to doom.

JOHN STERLING.

THE SEA.

THE sea ! the sea ! the open sea !
   The blue, the fresh, the ever free !
Without a mark, without a bound,
It runneth the earth's wide regions round ;
It plays with the clouds ; it mocks the skies ;
Or like a cradled creature lies.

I'm on the sea ! I'm on the sea !
I am where I would ever be ;
With the blue above, and the blue below,
And silence wheresoe'er I go ;
If a storm should come and awake the deep,
What matter ? I shall ride and sleep.

I love, oh how I love to ride
On the fierce, foaming, bursting tide,
When every mad wave drowns the moon,
Or whistles aloft his tempest tune,

And tells how goeth the world below,
And why the sou'west blasts do blow.

I never was on the dull, tame shore,
But I loved the great sea more and more,
And backward flew to her billowy breast,
Like a bird that seeketh its mother's nest ;
And a mother she was, and is, to me ;
For I was born on the open sea !

The waves were white, and red the morn,
In the noisy hour when I was born ;
And the whale it whistled, the porpoise rolled,
And the dolphins bared their backs of gold ;
And never was heard such an outcry wild
As welcomed to life the ocean-child !

I've lived since then, in calm and strife,
Full fifty summers, a sailor's life,
With wealth to spend, and power to range,
But never have sought nor sighed for change ;
And Death, whenever he comes to me,
Shall come on the wild, unbounded sea !

BARRY CORNWALL.

MOONLIGHT AT SEA.

IT is the midnight hour : the beauteous sea,
  Calm as the cloudless heaven, the heaven discloses ;
While many a sparkling star, in quiet glee,
  Far down within the watery sky reposes.

As if the ocean's heart were stirred
With inward life, a sound is heard,
Like that of dreamer murmuring in his sleep;
'Tis partly the billow, and partly the air,
That lies like a garment floating fair
  Above the happy deep.
The sea, I ween, cannot be fanned
By evening freshness from the land,
  For the land is far away;
But God hath willed that the sky-borne breeze
In the centre of the loneliest seas
  Should ever sport and play.
The mighty moon she sits above,
Encircled with a zone of love,
A zone of dim and tender light,
That makes her wakeful eye more bright:
She seems to shine with a sunny ray,
And the light looks like a mellowed day!
The gracious mistress of the main
Hath now an undisturbèd reign!
And from her silent throne looks down,
As upon children of her own,
On the waves that lend their gentle breast
In gladness for her couch of rest!

JOHN WILSON.

CALM AT SEA.

THE night is clear,
  The sky is fair,
The wave is resting on the ocean;

And far and near
The silent air
Just lifts the flag with faintest motion.

There is no gale
To fill the sail,
No wind to heave the curling billow;
The streamers droop
And trembling stoop,
Like boughs, that crown the weeping willow.

From off the shore
Is heard the roar
Of waves in softest motion rolling;
The twinkling stars
And whispering airs
Are all to peace the heart controlling.

The moon is bright,
Her ring of light,
In silver, pales the blue of heaven,
Or tints with gold,
Where lightly rolled,
Like fleecy snow, the rack is driven.

How calm and clear
The silent air!
How smooth and still the glassy ocean!
While stars above
Seem lamps of love,
To light the temple of devotion.

J. G. PERCIVAL.

FROM "THE BUCCANEER."

THE island lies nine leagues away.
　　Along its solitary shore,
Of craggy rock and sandy bay,
　　No sound but ocean's roar,
Save, where the bold, wild sea-bird makes her home,
Her shrill cry coming through the sparkling foam.

But when the light winds lie at rest,
　　And on the glassy, heaving sea,
The black duck, with her glossy breast,
　　Sits swinging silently;
How beautiful! no ripples break the reach,
And silvery waves go noiseless up the beach.

And inland rests the green, warm dell;
　　The brook comes tinkling down its side;
From out the trees the Sabbath bell
　　Rings cheerful far and wide,
Mingling its sound with bleatings of the flocks,
That feed about the vale among the rocks.

RICHARD H. DANA

OH, I love to be out by the waters at night,
　　As they trip to the sea on the bright-tinted
　　　　sands!
And deem their glad billows are children of light,
　　With songs on their lips and the stars in their hands.

ALICE CARY.

THE SKY IS THICK UPON THE SEA.

THE sky is thick upon the sea,
   The sea is sown with rain,
And in the passing gusts we hear
   The clanging of the crane.

The cranes are flying to the south ;
   We cut the northern foam :
The dreary land they leave behind
   Must be our future home.

Its barren shores are long and dark,
   And gray its autumn sky ;
But better these than this gray sea,
   If but to land — and die !

                              R. H. STODDARD.

OUT TO SEA.

THE wind is blowing east,
   And the waves are running free ;
Let's hoist the sail at once,
   And stand out to sea,
      (You and me !)
   I am growing more and more
   A-weary of the shore ;
   It was never so before, —
      Out to sea !

The wind is blowing east,
　　How it swells the straining sail !
A little farther out
　　We shall have a jolly gale !
　　　　(Cling to me !)
　　The waves are running high,
　　And the gulls, how they fly !
　　We shall only see the sky
　　　　Out to sea.

The wind is blowing east
　　From the dark and bloody shore,
Where flash a million swords,
　　And the dreadful cannon roar !
　　　　(Woe is me !)
　　There's a curse upon the land !
　　(Is that blood upon my hand ?)
　　What *can* we do but stand
　　　　Out to sea ?

　　　　　　　　　R. H. STODDARD.

NOONDAY BY THE SEASIDE.

THE sea has left the strand ;
　　In their deep sapphire cup
The waves lie gathered up,
Off the hard-ribbed sand.

From each dark rocky brim,
The full wine tinted billows ebbed away
　　Leave on the golden rim
Of their huge bowl not one thin line of spray.

Above the short-grassed downs all broidered over
With scarlet pimpernel and silver clover,
Like spicy incense quivers the warm air ;
  With piercing fervid heat
  The noonday sunbeams beat
On the red granite sea-slabs, broad and bare.
  And prone along the shore,
   Basking in the fierce glare,
  Lie sun-bronzed Titans, covered o'er
  With shaggy, sea-weed hair.

Come in, under this vault of brownest shade,
  By sea-worn arches made,
Where all the air, with a rich topaz light,
  Is darkly bright.
  'Neath these rock-folded canopies,
   Shadowy and cool,
  The crystal water lies
   In many a glassy pool,
Whose green-veined sides, as they receive the light,
Gleam like pale wells of precious malachite.

In the warm shallow water dip thy feet,
Gleaming like rose-hued pearls below the wave,
And lying in this hollow, sea-smoothed seat,
Gaze on the far-off white-sailed fisher fleet,
Framed in the twilight portal of our cave ;
  While I lie here, and gaze on thee.
  Fairer art thou to me
Than Aphrodite, when the breathless deep
Wafted her, smiling in her rosy sleep,

10

Towards the green-myrtled shore, that in delight,
With starry fragrance, suddenly grew white ;
　　Or than the shuddering girl,
　　Whose wide distended eyes,
　　Glassy, with dread surprise,
　　Saw the huge billow curl,
Foaming and bristling with its grisly freight ;
　　While, twinkling from afar,
With iris-feathered heels, and falchion bright,
From the blue copse of heaven's dazzling height,
Her lover swooped, a flashing noon-tide star.

A mid-day dream hath lighted on thy brow,
And gently bends it down ; thy fair eyes swim,
In liquid languor, lustreless and dim ;
And slowly dropping now,
From the light loosened clasp of thy warm hand,
Making a ruddy shadow on the sand,
Falls a wine-perfumed rose, with crimson glow.

Sleep, my beloved ! while the sultry spell
Of silent noon o'er sea and earth doth dwell ;
Stoop thy fair graceful head upon my breast,
With its thick rolls of golden hair opprest,
My lily ! — and my breathing shall not sob
With one tumultuous sigh, nor my heart throb
With one irregular bound, that I may keep,
With tenderest watch, the treasure of thy sleep.
Droop gently down, in slumb'rous, slow eclipse,
Fair fringèd lids ! beneath my sealing lips.

'FRANCES ANNE KEMBLE.

SEA-TANGLE.

"GO show to earth your power!" the East
        Wind cried
Commanding ; and the swift, submissive seas,
In ordered files, like liquid mountains, glide,
    Moving from sky to sky with godlike ease.

Its march sublime was as a lifting world
    Subsiding into glassy valleys vast :
No crest of foam upon its brow was curled ;
    But silent, dark, and terrible, it passed.

Below a cliff, where mused a little maid,
    It struck.   Its voice in thunder cried, "Be-
        ware ! "
But, to delight her, instantly displayed
    A fount of showering diamonds in the air.

" Go, cruel thing ! " she said, " unloved by me ;
    Go, tear the sailor from his happy sleep ;
Drown navies in thy heartless perfidy ;
    But spare our flowers, thou monster of the
        deep ! "

As in obedience, the wave passed on,
    Touching each shore with silver-sandalled feet,
But tossed, in flying, in the sun which shone,
    A handful to her lap of sea-blooms sweet.

More delicate than forms the frost doth weave
   On window-panes, are Ocean's filmy brood;
Remembering the awful home they leave,
   Their hues to that dim under-world subdued.

Fair spread on pages white, I saw arrayed
   These fairy-children of a sire so stern:
Their beauty charmed me; while the little maid
   Spoke of her new-found love with cheeks which
         burn, —

" So grand, so terrible, how could I know
   He cared for these ? " she faltered, — "darlings
         dear !
That his great heart could nurture them, and glow
   With such a love beneath such look severe ? "

Like God, the Ocean, too, the least can heed,
   Yearn iu a moon-led quest to farthest shores,
And fondle in delight its smallest weed,
   Yet look to Him it mirrors and adores.

T. G. APPLETON.

THE SHORE.

CAN it be women that walk in the sea-mist under the
   cliffs there ?
Where, 'neath a briny bow, creaming advances the lip
Of the foam, and out from the sand-choked anchors on
   to the skiffs there
The long ropes swing through the surge as it tumbles,
   and glitter and drip.

All the place, in a lurid glimmering emerald glory,
Glares like a Titan world come back under heaven
    again ;
Yonder, up there, are the steeps of the sea-kings
    famous in story,
But who are they on the beach ?   They are neither
. women nor men.

Who knows.   Are they the land's or the water's
    living creatures ?
Born of the boiling sea ? nursed in the seething
    storms ?
With their woman's hair dishevelled over their stern
    male features,
Striding bare to the knee, magnified maritime forms !

They may be the mothers and wives, they may be the
    sisters and daughters,
Of men in the dark mid-seas, alone in those black-
    coil'd hulls,
That toil 'neath yon white cloud, whence the moon will
    rise o'er the waters
To-night with her face on fire, if the wind in the even-
    ing lulls.

But they may be merely visions, such as only sick men
    witness
(Sitting, as I sit here, filled with a wild regret),
Framed from the sea's misshapen spume with a horri-
    ble fitness
To the winds in which they walk, and the surges by
    which they are wet.

Salamanders, sea-wolves, witches, warlocks, marine-
    monsters,
Which the dying seaman beholds when the rats are
    swimming away,
And an Indian wind 'gins hiss from an unknown isle,
    and alone stirs
The broken cloud which burns on the verge of the dead
    red day.

I know not.   All my mind is confused, nor can I dis-
    sever
The mould of the visible world from the shape of my
    thoughts in me.
The Inward and Outward are fused, and through them
    murmur for ever
The sorrow whose sound is the wind, and the roar of
    the limitless sea.

OWEN MEREDITH.

ON THE CLIFF.

I.

I LEANED on the turf,
    I looked at a rock
Left dry by the surf;
For the turf, to call it grass were to mock:
Dead to the roots, so deep was done
The work of the summer sun.

II.

And the rock lay flat
As an anvil's face :
No iron like that !
Baked dry : of a weed, of a shell, no trace ;
Sunshine outside, but ice at the core,
Death's altar by the lone shore.

III.

On the turf, sprang gay
With his films of blue,
No cricket, I'll say,
But a war-horse, barded and chanfroned too,
The gift of a quixote-mage to his knight,
Real fairy, with wings all right.

IV.

On the rock, they scorch
Like a drop of fire
From a brandished torch,
Fell two red fans of a butterfly :
No turf, no rock, — in their ugly stead,
See, wonderful blue and red !

V.

Is it not so
With the minds of men ?
The level and low,
The burnt and bare, in themselves ; but then
With such a blue and red grace, not theirs,
Love settling unawares !

ROBERT BROWNING.

THE SEA-LIMITS.

CONSIDER the sea's listless chime :
    Time's self it is made audible, —
The murmur of the earth's own shell.
Secret continuance sublime
    Is the sea's end.   Our sight may pass
    No furlong further.   Since time was,
This sound hath told the lapse of time.

No quiet which is death's, — it hath
    The mournfulness of ancient life,
    Enduring always at dull strife.
As the world's heart of rest and wrath,
    Its painful pulse is in the sands.
    Lost utterly, the whole sky stands
Gray and not known along its path.

Listen alone beside the sea,
    Listen alone among the woods ;
    Those voices of twin solitudes
Shall have one sound alike to thee.
    Hark where the murmurs of thronged men
    Surge and sink back and surge again, —
Still the one voice of wave and tree.

Gather a shell from the strewn beach,
    And listen at its lips : they sigh
    The same desire and mystery,

The echo of the whole sea's speech.
　　And all mankind is thus at heart
　　Not any thing but what thou art;
And Earth, Sea, Man, are all in each.

DANTE GABRIEL ROSSETTI.

CHILD'S SONG IN WINTER.

OUTSIDE the garden
　　The wet skies harden;
The gates are barred on
　　The summer side;
Shut out the flower time,
Sunbeam and shower time;
Make way for our time,
　　The winter tide.
Green once and cheery,
The woods worn weary,
Sigh as the dreary,
　　Weak sun goes home;
A great wind grapples
The wave, and dapples
The dead green floor of the sea with foam.

　　Through fell and moorland,
　　And salt sea foreland,
　　Our noisy norland
　　　　Resounds and rings;

Waste waves thereunder
Are blown in sunder,
And winds make thunder
 With cloud-wide wings.
Sea drift makes dimmer
The beacon's glimmer ;
Nor sail nor swimmer
 Can try the tides ;
And snow-drifts thicken
Where, when leaves quicken,
Under the heather the sundew hides.

In fierce March weather
White waves break tether,
And whirled together
 At either hand,
Like weeds uplifted,
The tree trunks rifted
In spars are drifted,
 Like foam or sand,
Past swamp and sallow,
And reed-beds callow,
Through pool and shallow,
 To wind and lee,
Till, no more tongue-tied,
Full flood and young tide
Roar down the rapids and storm the sea.

As men's cheeks faded
On shores invaded,
When shorewards waded
 The lords of fight ;

When churl and craven
Saw hard on haven
The wide-winged raven
 At main-mast height ;
When monks affrighted
To windward sighted
The birds full flighted
 Of swift sea-kings ;
So earth turns paler
When Storm, the sailor,
Steers in with a roar in the race of his wings.

O strong sea sailor,
Whose cheek turns paler
For wind or hail, or
 For fear of thee ?
O far sea-farer,
O thunder-bearer,
Thy songs are rarer
 Than soft songs be.
O fleet-foot stranger,
O North-Sea ranger,
Through days of danger
 And ways of fear,
Blow thy horn here for us,
Blow the sky clear for us,
Send us the song of the sea to hear.

Roll the strong stream of it
Up, till the scream of it
Wake from a dream of it

Children that sleep ;
Seamen that fare for them
Forth, with a prayer for them ;
Shall not God care for them ?
Angels not keep ?
Spare not the surges
Thy stormy scourges ;
Spare us the dirges
Of wives that weep.
Turn back the waves for us :
Dig no fresh graves for us :
Wind, in the manifold gulfs of the deep.

O stout north-easter,
Sea-king, land-waster,
For all thine haste, or
Thy stormy skill,
Yet hadst thou never,
For all endeavor,
Strength to dissever
Or strength to spill,
Save of His giving
Who gave our living,
Whose hands are weaving
What ours fulfil ;
Whose feet tread under
The storms and thunder ;
Who made our wonder to work His will.

His years and hours,
His world's blind powers,
His stars and flowers,

His nights and days,
Sea-tide and river,
And waves that shiver,
Praise God, the giver
 Of tongues to praise.
Winds in their blowing,
And fruits in growing,
Time in its going,
 While time shall be ;
In death and living,
With one thanksgiving,
Praise Him whose hand is the strength of the sea.

ALGERNON C. SWINBURNE.

SITTING ON THE SHORE.

THE tide has ebb'd away ;
 No more wild dashings 'gainst the adamant rocks,
Nor swayings amidst sea-weed false that mocks
 The hues of gardens gay ;
 No laugh of little wavelets at their play :
No lucid pools reflecting heaven's clear brow, —
Both storm and calm alike are ended now.

 The rocks sit gray and lone :
The shifting sand is spread so smooth and dry,
That not a tide might ever have swept by,
 Stirring it with rude moan :
 Only some weedy fragments, idly thrown
To rot beneath the sky, tell what has been ;
But Desolation's self has grown serene.

Afar the mountains rise,
And the broad estuary widens out,
All sunshine ; wheeling round and round about
    Seaward, a white bird flies.
    A bird ?   Nay, seems it rather in these eyes
A spirit, o'er Eternity's dim sea
Calling, — " Come thou where all we glad souls be."

    O life, O silent shore,
Where we sit patient ; O great sea beyond,
To which we turn with solemn hope and fond,
    But sorrowful no more !
    A little while, and then we too shall soar
Like while-wing'd sea-birds into the Infinite Deep :
Till then, Thou, Father, wilt our spirits keep.

DINAH MARIA MULOCH.

AT SEA.

WE part as ships on a pathless main,
    Gayly enough, for the sense of pain
Is asleep at first ; but ghosts will arise
    When we would repose, and the forms will come
    And walk when we walk, and will not be dumb,
Nor yet forget with their wakeful eyes.

When we most need rest, and the perfect sleep,
Some hand will reach from the dark, and keep

The curtains drawn and the pillows toss'd
  Like a tide of foam ; and one will say
  At night, — O Heaven, that it were day !
  And one by night through the misty tears
  Will say, — O Heaven, the days are years,
And I would to Heaven that the waves were cross'd.

JOAQUIN MILLER.

I STAND BESIDE THE MOBILE SEA.

I STAND beside the mobile sea ;
  And sails are spread, and sails are furl'd
From farthest corners of the world,
And fold like white wings wearily.
Steamships go up, and some go down
In haste, like traders in a town,
And seem to see and beckon all.
Afar at sea some white shapes flee,
With arms stretch'd like a ghost's to me,
And cloud-like sails far blown and curl'd
Then glide down to the under-world.
As if blown bare in winter blasts
Of leaf and limb, tall naked masts
Are rising from the restless sea,
So still and desolate and tall,
I seem to see them gleam and shine
With clinging drops of dripping brine.
Broad still brown wings flit here and there,
Thin sea-blue wings wheel everywhere,
And white wings whistle through the air :
I hear a thousand sea-gulls call.

Behold the ocean on the beach
Kneel lowly down as if in prayer.
I hear a moan as of despair,
While far at sea do toss and reach
Some things so like white pleading hands.
The ocean's thin and hoary hair
Is trail'd along the silver'd sands
At every sigh and sounding moan.
'Tis not a place for mirthfulness,
But meditation deep, and prayer,
And kneelings on the salted sod,
Where man must own his littleness
And know the mightiness of God.

JOAQUIN MILLER.

SURF.

SPLENDORS of morning the billow-crests brighten,
    Lighting and luring them on to the land, —
Far away waves where the wan vessels whiten,
    Blue rollers breaking in surf where we stand.
Curved like the necks of a legion of horses,
    Each with his froth-gilded mane flowing free,
Hither they speed in perpetual courses,
    Bearing thy riches, O beautiful sea!

Strong with the striving of yesterday's surges,
    Lashed by the wanton winds leagues from the shore,
Each, driven fast by its follower, urges
    Fearlessly those that are fleeting before;

How they leap over the ridges we walk on,
 Flinging us gifts from the depths of the sea, —
Silvery fish for the foam-haunting falcon,
 Palm-weed and pearls for my darling and me !

Light falls her foot where the rift follows after,
 Finer her hair than your feathery spray,
Sweeter her voice than your infinite laughter, —
 Hist ! ye wild couriers, list to my·lay !
Deep in the chambers of grottos auroral
 Morn laves her jewels and bends her red knee :
Thence to my dear one your amber and coral
 Bring for her dowry, O beautiful sea !

Edmund Clarence Stedman.

A THANKSGIVING.

HIGH on the ledge the wind blows the bay-berry
  bright,
Turning the leaves till they shudder and shine in the
  light :
Yellow St. John's-wort and yarrow are nodding their
  heads.
Iris and wild-rose are glowing in purples and reds.

Swift flies the schooner careering beyond o'er the
  blue ;
Faint shows the furrow she leaves as she cleaves
  lightly through ;
Gay gleams the fluttering flag at her delicate mast,
Full swell the sails with the wind that is following
  fast.

Quail and sand-piper, and swallow and sparrow, are
    here ;
Sweet sound their manifold notes, high and low, far
    and near ;
Chorus of musical waters, the rush of the breeze,
Steady and strong from the South, — what glad voices
    are these !

O cup of the wild-rose, curved close to hold odorous
    dew,
What thought do you hide in your heart ?   I would
    that I knew !
O beautiful Iris, unfurling your purple and gold,
What victory fling you abroad in the flags you unfold !

Sweet may your thought be, red rose ; but still sweeter
    is mine,
Close in my heart hidden, clear as your dewdrop
    divine.
Flutter your gonfalons, Iris, — the pæan I sing
Is for victory better than joy or than beauty can bring.

Into thy calm eyes, O Nature, I look and rejoice ;
Prayerful, I add my one note to the Infinite voice :
As shining and singing and sparkling glides on the
    glad day,
And eastward the swift-rolling planet wheels into the
    gray.

CELIA THAXTER.

DOWN ON THE SHORE.

DOWN on the shore, on the sunny shore !
    Where the salt smell cheers the land ;
Where the tide moves bright under boundless light,
    And the surge on the glittering strand ;
Where the children wade in the shallow pools,
    Or run from the froth in play ;
Where the swift little boats with milk-white wings
    Are crossing the sapphire bay,
And the ship in full sail, with a fortunate gale,
    Holds proudly on her way.
    Where the nets are spread on the grass to dry,
And asleep, hard by, the fishermen lie,
Under the tent of the warm blue sky,
    With the hushing wave on its golden floor
    To sing their lullaby.

Down on the shore, on the stormy shore !
    Beset by a growling sea,
Whose mad waves leap on the rocky steep,
    Like wolves up a traveller's tree.
Where the foam flies wide, and an angry blast
    Blows the curlew off with a screech ;
Where the brown sea-wrack, torn up by the roots,
    Is flung out of fishes' reach ;
Where the tall ship rolls on the hidden shoals,
    And scatters her planks on the beach.

Where slate and straw through the village spin,
And a cottage fronts the fiercest din,
With a sailor's wife sitting sad within,
  Hearkening the wind and water's roar,
    Till at last her tears begin.

                              WILLIAM ALLINGHAM.

BY THE MORNING SEA.

THE wind shakes up the sleepy clouds
    To kiss the ruddied morn,
And from their awful misty shrouds
  The mountains are new-born :
The sea lies fresh with open eyes ;
  Night-fears and moaning dreams,
Brooding like clouds on nether skies,
  Have sunk below, and beams
Dance on the floor like golden flies,
  Or strike with joyful gleams
Some white-winged ship, a wandering star
Of ocean, piloting afar.

In brakes, in woods, in cottage-eaves,
  The early birds are rife,
Quick voices thrill the sprinkled leaves
  In ecstasy of life ;
With silent gratitude of flowers
  The morning's breath is sweet,
And cool with dew, that freshly showers
  Round wild things' hasty feet.

But the heavenly guests of tranquil hours
  To inner skies retreat,
From human thoughts of lower birth
That stir upon the waking earth.

Across a thousand leagues of land
  The mighty sun looks free,
And in their fringe of rock or sand
  A thousand leagues of sea.
Lo ! I, in this majestic room,
  As real as the sun,
Inherit this day and its doom
  Eternally begun.
A world of men the rays illume,
  God's men, and I am one.
But life that is not pure and bold
Doth tarnish every morning's gold.

WILLIAM ALLINGHAM.

WAITING BY THE SEA.

ALONE upon the windy hills
  I stand and face the open sea,
And drink the southern breeze that fills
  The sails that bring my love to me.

Far out the shores and woodlands reach,
  Till lost in mists of pearly gray,
Or crossed by lines of yellow beach
  And flashing breakers far away.

Alone upon the windy slopes,
   I watch the long, blue, level wall
Of ocean, where my winged hopes,
   Like fluttering sea-birds, fly and call.

O happy pilot-boats that dance
   Across the sparkling miles of sea,
O greet her, should ye meet by chance
   The ship that bears my love to me !

And does she lean upon the deck,
   And strain her eyes till land appears,
As I to catch the white-winged speck
   That clears away my gathering fears ?

By long, low beach and wooded crag
   The crowded sails go glimmering past ;
But none that bear the well-known flag
   And pennon streaming from the mast.

O ocean, wrinkling in the sun !
   O breeze, that blowest from the sea !
Waft into port, ere day is done,
   My love, my life, again to me !

She comes, she comes ! I see the sails,
   Like rounded sea-shells full and white ;
I hear the booming gun that hails
   The coming of my heart's delight.

I hear the sailors' distant song,
   They crowd the deck in bustling glee;
And there is one amid the throng
   Who waves a rosy scarf to me.

The sun has set, the air is still,
   The twilight reddens o'er the sea,
The full moon rises o'er the hill,
   But joy like sunrise shines for me.

C. P. CRANCH.

THE MUSIC OF THE SEA.

From "The Golden Legend."

THE night is calm and cloudless,
   And still as still can be,
And the stars come forth to listen
   To the music of the sea.
They gather, and gather, and gather,
   Until they crowd the sky,
And listen, in breathless silence,
   To the solemn litany.
It begins in rocky caverns,
   As a voice that chants alone
To the pedals of the organ
   In monotonous undertone;
And anon from shelving beaches,
   And shallow sands beyond,
In snow-white robes uprising,
   The ghostly choirs respond.

And sadly and unceasing
   The mournful voice sings on,
And the snow-white choirs still answer,
   Christe eleison !

Henry W. Longfellow.

OUT AT SEA.

FAR on the deep mid-ocean tossed,
   Leagues away from the friendly shore,
In the watery wilderness lost,
   Driven and deafened by rush and roar,
Baffled by wind and wave are we ; —
What sweet home-spirits may there be,
Sadly pondering on our wandering
   Wide and wearisome, out at sea !

Lying here in my tossing bed,
   I dream of ruin, and rock, and wreck, —
Hearing the slow, continuous tread
   Of the sailor who walks the deck,
Keeping his long watch patiently ; —
Gentler watchers on shore there be ;
Eyes which weep for us, leaving sleep for us,
   Fond watch keep for us, out at sea !

In at the narrow window there
   Drifts the ocean wind, wild and damp,
Frightening into flicker and flare
   The feeble flame of the swinging lamp ;

Yet, though lonesome and dark it be,
There are places where steadily
Faith's fires burn for us, true hearts mourn for us,
   Dear arms yearn for us, out at sea !

Blinded and beaten by wind and foam,
   Hurled and tossed at the sea's command,
Sweet the thought that in some dear home,
   Steady and still on the solid land,
Where our hopes and our memories be
Safely harbored from storm and sea,
Love takes heed for us, love's lips plead for us,
   Love's prayers speed for us, out at sea!

Night and darkness, and storm and clouds ;
   Creak of cordage and shudder of sails ;
Drifting drearily through the shrouds,
   There is a murmur of mournful wails, —
Dirges sung for the lost at sea,
Where the tempest is fierce and free :
Father, hear to us, bend Thine ear to us,
   Be thou near to us, out at sea !

ELIZABETH AKERS.

ON THE SEA.

THE pathway of the sinking moon
   Fades from the silent bay ;
The mountain-isles loom large and faint,
   Folded in shadows gray,
And the lights of land are setting stars
   That soon will pass away.

O boatman, cease thy mellow song !
　O minstrel, drop thy lyre !
Let us hear the voice of the midnight sea,
　Let us speak as the waves inspire,
While the plashy dip of the languid oar
　Is a furrow of silver fire.

Day cannot make thee half so fair,
　Nor the stars of eve so dear ;
The arms that clasp and the breast that keeps,
　They tell me thou art near,
And the perfect beauty of thy face
　In thy murmured words I hear.

The lights of land have dropped below
　The vast and glimmering sea ;
The world we leave is a tale that is told, —
　A fable that cannot be.
There is no life in the sphery dark
　But the love in thee and me !

BAYARD TAYLOR.

FROM "THE BATH."

WHERE yonder dancing billows dip,
　　Far-off, to ocean's misty verge,
Ploughs Morning, like a full-sailed ship,
　　The orient's cloudy surge.

With spray of scarlet fire before
  The ruffled gold that round her dies,
She sails above the sleeping shore,
  Across the waking skies.

The dewy beach beneath her glows ;
  A pencilled beam, the lighthouse burns :
Full-breathed, the fragrant sea-wind blows, —
  Life to the world returns !

BAYARD TAYLOR.

SUNKEN TREASURES.

WHEN the uneasy waves of life subside,
  And the soothed ocean sleeps in glassy rest,
I see submerged, beyond or storm or tide,
  The treasures gathered in its greedy breast.

There still they shine through the translucent Past,
  Far down on that forever quiet floor ;
No fierce upheaval of the deep shall cast
  Them back, no wave shall wash them to the shore.

I see them gleaming beautiful as when
  Erewhile they floated, convoys of my fate;
The barks of lovely women, noble men,
  Full sailed with hope, and stored with Love's own
    freight.

The sunken treasures of my heart as well
   Look up to me as perfect as at dawn ;
My golden palace heaves beneath the swell
   To meet my touch, and is again withdrawn.

There sleep the early triumphs, cheaply won,
   That led Ambition to his utmost verge ;
And still his visions, like a drowning sun,
   Send up receding splendors through the surge.

There wait the recognitions, the quick ties,
   Whence the heart knows its kin wherever cast ;
And there the partings, when the wistful eyes
   Caress each other, as they look their last.

There lie the summer eves, delicious eves,
   The soft green valleys drenched with light divine,
The lisping murmurs of the chestnut leaves,
   The hand that lay, the eyes that looked in mine.

There lives the hour of fear and rapture yet,
   The perilled climax of the passionate years ;
There still the rains of wan December wet
   A naked mound, — I cannot see for tears.

I see them all, but stretch my hands in vain ;
   No deep sea plummet reaches where they rest ;
No cunning diver shall descend the main
   And bring a single jewel from its breast.

BAYARD TAYLOR.

LOW TIDE.

UNDER the cliff I walk in silence,
　　While the intrepid waters flow,
And the white birds, lit by the sun into silver,
　　Glitter against the blue below ;
　　　　And the tide is low.

Here, years ago, in golden weather,
　　Under the cliff, and close to the sea,
A pledge was given that made me master
　　Of all that ever was dear to me ;
　　　　And the tide was low.

Only a little year fled by after,
　　Then my bride and I came once more,
And saw the sea, like a bird imprisoned,
　　Beating its wings 'gainst its bars, the shore ;
　　　　And the tide was low.

Now I walk alone by the filmy breakers, —
　　A voice is hushed I can never forget ;
Upon my sea dead calm has fallen,
　　My ships are harbored, my sun is set ;
　　　　And the tide is low.

　　　　　　　　　　Henry Abbey.

DONALD.

O MY white, white, light moon, that sailest in the
sky,
Look down upon the whirling world, for thou art up so
high,
And tell me where my Donald is who sailed across the
sea,
And make a path of silver light to lead him back to
me.

O my white, white, bright moon, thy cheek is coldly
fair,
A little cloud beside thee seems thy wildly floating
hair ;
And if thou wouldst not have me grow as white and
cold as thee,
Go, make a mighty tide to draw my Donald back to
me.

O my light, white, bright moon, that doth so fondly
shine,
There is not a lily in the world but hides its face from
thine ;
I too shall go and hide my face close in the dust from
thee,
Unless with light and tide thou bring my Donald back
to me.

HENRY ABBEY.

THE LAND-SICK.

GREEN fields are about me with hill and plain,
  And corn on the upland lea ;
I long for the blue and billowy main,
And instead of these harvests of waving grain
  For the roll and the surf of the sea.

The swallow is twittering my window by,
  And carols his summer song ;
'Twere better aloft on the tops to lie,
While the gull and the sea-mew around me fly,
  Still swooping and circling along.

I hear the laugh and the revelling shout
  Of the jocund boys at play ;
But the silvery dolphin seems sporting about,
And I think how the pirate bonita leaps out
  For its reckless and fugitive prey.

With their "church-going bells," my ears they tire,
  And weary is service time ;
Give me the tall mast for the tapering spire,
And the high-piping winds for the pealing choir,
  With the dash of the waves to chime !

They point to the woodlands, and rocks so gray
  With their shadows ere twilight's begun ;
One hour of the sea-cradled dying of day,
With a phantom-like sail in the distance away,
  Is enough for my mother's son !

And then, when the broad harvest-moon one sees
    Climb up in the eastern sky,
He thinks what bright watches on deck are these,
With the mizzen-top-gallant swelled full by the breeze,
    And the star-spangled waves dancing by.

They call this home, and they whisper me
    That my thoughts are but truants now;
But there's many a home o'er the deep blue sea,
And love-lit eyes 'neath the banyan-tree
    Or the shade of the orange-bough!

E. W. B. CANNING.

BY THE SEA.

SLOWLY, steadily, under the moon,
    Swings the tide, in its old-time way;
Never too late, and never too soon, —
    And the evening and morning make the day.

Slowly, steadily, over the sands,
    And over the rocks, to fall and flow,
And this wave has touched a dead man's hands,
    And that one has seen a face we know.

They have borne the good ship on her way,
    Or buried her deep from love and light;
And yet, as they sink at our feet to-day,
    Ah, who shall interpret their message aright?

For their separate voices of grief and cheer
   Are blending at last in one solemn tone;
And only this song of the waves I hear,
   " Forever and ever His will is done!"

Slowly, steadily, to and fro,
   Swings our life in its weary way;
Now at its ebb, and now at its flow, —
   And the evening and morning make the day.

Sorrow and happiness, peace and strife,
   Fear and rejoicing, its moments know, —
How, from the discords of such a life,
   Can the clear music of heaven flow?

Yet to the ear of God it swells,
   And to the blessed round the throne,
Sweeter than chimes of Sabbath bells, —
   " Forever and ever His will is done!"

ANON.

BY THE SEA.

I WALKED with her I love by the sea.
   The deep came up with its chanting waves,
Making a music so great and free
That the will and the faith, which were dead in me,
   Awoke and rose from their graves.

Chanting, and with a regal sweep
  Of their 'broidered garments up and down
The strand, came the mighty waves of the deep,
  Dragging the wave-worn drift from its sleep
    Along the sea-sands bare and brown.

" O my soul, make the song of the sea ! " I cried.
  " How it comes, with its stately tread,
And its dreadful voice, and the splendid pride
  Of its regal garments flowing wide
    Over the land ! " to my soul I said.

My soul was still ; the deep went down.
  " What hast thou, my soul," I cried,
" In thy song ? "   " The sea-sands bare and brown,
  With broken shells and sea-weed strown,
    And stranded drift," my soul replied.

W. D. Howells.

BUBBLES.

I.

I STOOD on the brink in childhood,
  And watched the bubbles go
From the rock-fretted, sunny ripple
  To the smoother tide below ;

And over the white creek-bottom,
  Under them every one,
Went golden stars in the water,
  All luminous with the sun.

But the bubbles broke on the surface ;
　　And under, the stars of gold
Broke ; and the hurrying water
　　Flowed onward, swift and cold.

II.

I stood on the brink in manhood,
　　And it came to my weary brain,
And my heart, so dull and heavy
　　After the years of pain, —

That every hollowest bubble
　　Which over my life had passed
Still into its deeper current
　　Some heavenly gleam had cast ;

That, however I mocked it gayly,
　　And guessed at its hollowness,
Still shone, with each bursting bubble,
　　One star in my soul the less.

W. D. Howrlls.

PLEASURE-PAIN.

I.

ONE sails away to sea,
　　One stands on the shore and cries ;
The ship goes down the world, and the light
　　On the sullen water dies.

The whispering shell is mute,
  And after is evil cheer:
She shall stand on the shore and cry in vain
  Many and many a year.

But the stately, wide-winged ship
  Lies wrecked on the unknown deep;
Far under, dead in his coral bed,
  The lover lies asleep.

II.

Like a bird of evil presage,
  To the lonely house on the shore
Came the wind with a tale of shipwreck,
  And shrieked at the bolted door,

And flapped its wings in the gables,
  And shouted the well-known names,
And buffeted the windows
  Afeard in their shuddering frames.

It was night, and it is morning, —
  The summer sun is bland,
The white-cap waves come rocking, rocking
  In to the summer land.

The white-cap waves come rocking, rocking
  In the sun so soft and bright,
And toss and play with the dead man
  Drowned in the storm last night.

                              W. D. HOWELLS.

THE SEA.

IT surged and foamed on cold gray lands,
 No life was in its waves :
It rolled and raged on barren strands,
 Or thundered into caves ;
And yet it sang a glorious song,
An ancient pæan loud and long.

It broke upon the new-made beach,
 That roaring, restless Sea,
The only burden of its speech
 One word, — Eternity ;
And ever sang that glorious song,
An ancient pæan loud and long.

EDMUND SANDARS,

SONG OF THE DANISH SEA-KING.

OUR bark is on the waters deep, our bright blade's
 in our hand,
Our birthright is the ocean vast, — we scorn the
 girdled land ;
And the hollow wind is our music brave, and none
 can bolder be
Than the hoarse-tongued tempest raving o'er a proud
 and swelling sea !

Our bark is dancing on the waves, its tall masts
    quivering bend
Before the gale, which hails us now with the hollo of a
    friend ;
And its prow is sheering merrily the upcurled billow's
    foam,
While our hearts, with throbbing gladness, cheer old
    Ocean as our home.

Our eagle wings of might we stretch before the gallant
    wind,
And we leave the tame and sluggish earth a dim mean
    speck behind ;
We shoot into the untracked deep, as earth-freed
    spirits soar,
Like stars of fire through boundless space, — through
    realms without a shore !

Lords of this wide-spread wilderness of waters, we
    bound free,
The haughty elements alone dispute our sovereignty ;
No landmark doth our freedom let, for no law of man
    can mete
The sky which arches o'er our head, the waves which
    kiss our feet !

The warrior of the land may back the wild horse, in
    his pride ;
But a fiercer steed we dauntless breast, — the untamed
    ocean tide ;

And a nobler tilt our bark careers, as it quells the
    saucy wave,
While the herald storm peals o'er the deep the glories
    of the brave.

Hurrah ! hurrah ! the wind is up, — it bloweth fresh
    and free,
And every cord instinct with life pipes loud its fear-
    less glee ;
Big swell the bosomed sails with joy, and they madly
    kiss the spray,
As proudly, through the foaming surge, the Sea-King
    bears away !

WILLIAM MOTHERWELL.

WEEL MAY THE BOATIE ROW.

WEEL may the boatie row, and better may it
    speed,
Weel may the boatie row that gains the bairnies' bread.
The boatie rows, the boatie rows, the boatie rows fu'
    weel,
And mickle luck attend the boat, the merlin, and the
    creel.

I cast my line in Largo Bay, and fishes I caught nine ;
Three to boil, and three to fry, and three to bait the
    line.
The boatie rows, the boatie rows, the boatie rows
    indeed,
And happy be the lot of a' who wishes her to speed.

When Sawnie, Jock, and Janetie are up and gotten
    lear,
They'll help to gar the boatie row, and lighten all our
    care.
The boatie rows, the boatie rows, the boatie rows fu'
    weel,
And lightsome be her heart that bears the merlin and
    the creel.

And when wi' age we're worn down, and hirpling at
    the door,
They'll row to keep us dry and warm, as we did them
    before.
The boatie rows, the boatie rows, the boatie rows
    indeed,
And happy be the lot of a' that wish the boat to speed.

John Ewen.

TOO LONG, O SPIRIT OF STORM.

TOO long, O spirit of Storm,
    Thy lightning sleeps in its sheath !
I am sick to the soul of yon pallid sky,
    And the moveless sea beneath.

Come down in thy strength on the deep !
    Worse dangers there are in life,
When the waves are still, and the skies look fair,
    Than in their wildest strife.

A friend I knew, whose days
    Were as calm as this sky overhead ;
But one blue morn that was fairest of all,
    The heart in his bosom fell dead.

And they thought him alive while he walked
    The streets that he walked in youth, —
Ah! little they guessed the seeming man
    Was a soulless corpse in sooth.

Come down in thy strength, O Storm !
    And lash the deep till it raves !
I am sick to the soul of that quiet sea,
    Which hides ten thousand graves.

HENRY TIMROD.

STORM–SONG.

THE clouds are scudding across the moon,
    A misty light is on the sea ;
The wind in the shrouds has a wintry tune,
    And the foam is flying free.

Brothers, a night of terror and gloom
    Speaks in the cloud and gathering roar :
Thank God, He has given us broad sea-room,
    A thousand miles from shore.

Down with the hatches on those who sleep !
    The wild and whistling deck have we :
Good watch, my brothers, to-night we'll keep,
    While the tempest is on the sea !

Though the rigging shriek in his terrible grip,
    And the naked spars be snapped away,
Lashed to the helm, we'll drive our ship
    In the teeth of the whelming spray!

Hark! how the surges o'erleap the deck!
    Hark! how the pitiless tempest raves!
Ah, daylight will look upon many a wreck
    Drifting over the desert waves.

Yet, courage, brothers! we trust the wave,
    With God above us, our guiding chart;
So, whether to harbor or ocean-grave,
    Be it still with a cheery heart!

BAYARD TAYLOR.

THE LONG WHITE SEAM.

A S I came round the harbor buoy,
    The lights began to gleam,
No wave the land-locked harbor stirred,
    The crags were white as cream;
And I marked my love by candle-light
    Sewing her long white seam.
        It's aye sewing ashore, my dear,
            Watch and steer at sea;
        It's reef and furl and haul the line,
            Set sail and think of thee.

I climbed to reach her cottage door ;
O sweetly my love sings ;
Like a shaft of light her voice breaks forth,
My soul to meet it springs,
As the shining water leaped of old,
When stirred by angel wings.
Aye longing to list anew,
Awake and in my dream ;
But never a song she sang like this,
Sewing her long white seam.

Fair fall the lights, the harbor lights
That brought me in to thee,
And peace drop down on that low roof
For the sight that I did see,
And the voice, my dear, that rang so clear,
All for the love of me.
For O, for O, with brows bent low,
By the candle's flickering gleam,
Her wedding gown it was she wrought,
Sewing the long white seam.

JEAN INGELOW.

THE SONG OF THE GALLEY.

From the Spanish.

I.

"YE mariners of Spain,
Bend strongly on your oars,
And bring my love again,
For he lies among the Moors.

II.

" Ye galleys fairly built
Like castles on the sea,
O great will be your guilt,
If ye bring him not to me.

III.

" The wind is blowing strong,
The breeze will aid your oars ;
O swiftly fly along,
For he lies among the Moors.

IV.

" The sweet breeze of the sea
Cools every cheek but mine :
Hot is its breath to me,
As I gaze upon the brine.

V.

" Lift up, lift up your sail,
And bend upon your oars ;
O lose not the fair gale,
For he lies among the Moors.

VI.

" It is a narrow strait,
I see the blue hills over ;
Your coming I'll await,
And thank you for my lover.

VII.

" To Mary I will pray,
    While ye bend upon your oars ;
'Twill be a blessed day,
    If ye fetch him from the Moors."

J. G. Lockhart.

BOAT-SONG.

O SWEET the flight at dead of night,
    When, up the immeasurable height,
The thin cloud wanders with the breeze
That shakes the splendor from the star,
That stoops and crisps the darkling seas
And drives the daring keel afar,
Where solitude and silence are !
To cleave the crested wave, and mark
Drowned in its depths the shattered spark,
On airy swells to soar and rise,
Where nothing but the foam-bell flies,
O'er freest tracks of wild delight, —
O sweet the flight at dead of night !

Harriet Prescott Spofford.

A MYTH.

A FLOATING, a floating
    Across the sleeping sea,
All night I heard a singing bird
    Upon the topmast tree.

" Oh, came you from the isles of Greece
　　Or from the banks of Seine ?
Or off some tree in forests free
　　That fringe the western main ? "

" I came not off the old world,
　　Nor yet from off the new ;
But I am one of the birds of God
　　Which sing the whole night through."

" Oh, sing and wake the dawning !
　　Oh, whistle for the wind !
The night is long, the current strong,
　　My boat it lags behind."

" The current sweeps the old world,
　　The current sweeps the new ;
The wind will blow, the dawn will glow,
　　Ere thou hast sailed them through."

C. KINGSLEY.

A LITTLE WHILE.

A LITTLE while, a little love
　　The hour yet bears for thee and me,
Who have not drawn the veil to see
　　If still our heaven be lit above.
Thou merely, at the day's last sigh,
　　Hast felt thy soul prolong the tone ;
And I have heard the night-wind cry,
　　And deemed its speech my own.

A little while, a little love
The scattering Autumn hoards for us,
Whose bower is not yet ruinous,
  Nor quite unleaved our songless grove.
Only across the shaken boughs
  We hear the flood-tides seek the sea,
And deep in both our hearts they rouse
  One wail for thee and me.

A little while, a little love
May yet be ours who have not said
The word it makes our eyes afraid
  To know that each is thinking of.
Not yet the end ; be our lips dumb
  In smiles a little season yet ;
I'll tell thee, when the end is come,
  How we may best forget.

DANTE GABRIEL ROSSETTI.

AGAIN ?

OH, sweet and fair !   Oh, rich and rare !
    That day so long ago.
The Autumn sunshine everywhere,
    The heather all aglow,
The ferns were clad in cloth of gold,
    The waves sang on the shore.
Such suns will shine, such waves will sing
    Forever evermore.

Oh, fit and few !   Oh, tried and true !
    The friends who met that day.
Each one the other's spirit knew,
    And so in earnest play
The hours flew past, until at last
    The twilight kissed the shore.
We said, " Such days shall come again
    Forever evermore."

One day again, no cloud of pain
    A shadow o'er us cast ;
And yet we strove in vain, in vain,
    To conjure up the past ;
Like, but unlike, — the sun that shone,
    The waves that beat the shore,
The words we said, the songs we sung,
    Like, — unlike, — evermore.

For ghosts unseen crept in between,
    And, when our songs flowed free,
Sang discords in an undertone,
    And marred our harmony.
"The past is ours, not yours," they said :
    " The waves that beat the shore,
Though like the same, are not the same,
    Oh, never, never more ! "

FRASER'S MAGAZINE.

THE SURVIVORS.

IN this sad hour, so still, so late,
  When flowers are dead and birds are flown,
Close-sheltered from the blasts of Fate,
  Our little love burns brightly on.

Amid the wrecks of dear desire
  That ride the waves of life no more;
As stranded voyagers light their fire
  Upon a lonely island shore.

And though we deem that, soft and fair,
  Beyond the tempest and the sea,
Our hearts' true homes are smiling, where
  In life we never more shall be, —

Yet we are saved, and we may rest;
  And, hearing each the other's voice,
We cannot hold ourselves unblest,
  Although we may not quite rejoice.

We'll warm our hearts and softly sing
  Thanks for the shore whereon we're driven;
Storm-tossed no more, we'll fold the wing,
  And dream forgotten dreams of heaven.

H. W. P.

THINE.

THE tide will ebb at day's decline.
   (Ich bin dein.)
Impatient for the open sea,
At anchor rocks the tossing ship, —
The ship that only waits for thee ;
Yet, with no tremble of the lip,
I say again, thy hand in mine,
    (Ich bin dein).

Too many clusters break the vine.
   (Ich bin dein.)   .
The tree whose strength and life outpour
In one exultant blossom-gush
Must flowerless be for evermore ;
We walk this way but once, friend, — hush !
Our feet have left no trodden line.
   (Ich bin dein.)

Who heaps his goblet wastes his wine.
   (Ich bin dein.)
The boat is moving from the land,
I have no chiding and no tears,
Now give me back my empty hand,
To battle with the cruel years !
Behold the triumph shall be mine !
   (Ich bin dein.)

ELIZABETH AKERS.

ALL THE RIVERS.

" ALL the rivers run into the sea."
  Like the pulsing of a river,
  The motion of a song,
  Wind the olden words along
The tortuous windings of my thought, whenever
   I sit beside the sea.

All the rivers run into the sea.
  O you little leaping river,
  Laugh on beneath your breath !
  With a heart as deep as death,
Strong stream, go patient, brave and hasting never,
   I sit beside the sea.

All the rivers run into the sea.
  Why the striving of a river,
  The passion of a soul ?
  Calm the eternal waters roll
Upon the eternal shore. Somewhere, whatever
   Seeks it finds the sea.

All the rivers run into the sea.
  O thou bounding, burning river,
  Hurrying heart ! — I seem
  To know (so one knows in a dream)
That in the waiting heart of God for ever
   Thou too shalt find the sea.

      ELIZABETH STUART PHELPS.

SONG.

IN the summer twilight,
  While yet the dew was hoar,
I went plucking purple pansies
  Till my love should come to shore.
The fishing-lights their dances
  Were keeping out at sea,
And " Come," I sang, " my true love,
  Come hasten home to me ! "

But the sea it fell a-moaning,
  And the white gulls rocked thereon,
And the young moon dropped from heaven,
  And the lights hid, one by one.
All silently their glances
  Slipped down the cruel sea,
And " Wait," cried the night and wind and
    storm,
  " Wait till I come to thee ! "

HARRIET PRESCOTT SPOFFORD.

"WHEN THE TIDE COMES IN."

WHEN the tide comes in,
    At once the shore and sea begin
Together to be glad.
  What the tide has brought
No man has asked, no man has sought:

What other tides have had
The deep sand hides away;
The last bit of the wrecks they wrought
Was burned up yesterday.

When the tide goes out,
The shore looks dark and sad with doubt.
The landmarks are all lost.
For the tide to turn
Men patient wait, men restless yearn.
Sweet channels they have crossed,
In boats that rocked with glee,
Stretch now bare stony roads, that burn
And lead away from sea.

When the tide comes in
In hearts, at once the hearts begin
Together to be glad.
What the tide has brought
They do not care, they have not sought.
All joy they ever had
The new joy multiplies;
All pain by which it may be bought
Seems paltry sacrifice.

When the tide goes out,
The hearts are wrung with fear and doubt:
All trace of joy seems lost.
Will the tide return?
In restless questioning they yearn.

With hands unclasped, uncrossed,
   They weep, on separate ways.
Ah ! darling, shall we ever learn
   Love's tidal hours and days ?

H. H.

SONG.

WE sail toward evening's lonely star,
   That trembles in the tender blue ;
One single cloud, a dusky bar,
   Burnt with dull carmine through and through,
Slow smouldering in the summer sky,
   Lies low along the fading west ;
How sweet to watch its splendors die,
   Wave-cradled thus, and wind-caressed !

The soft breeze freshens ; leaps the spray
   To kiss our cheeks with sudden cheer.
Upon the dark edge of the bay
   Lighthouses kindle far and near,
And through the warm deeps of the sky
   Steal faint star-clusters, while we rest
In deep refreshment, thou and I,
   Wave-cradled thus, and wind-caressed.

How like a dream are earth and heaven,
   Star-beam and darkness, sky and sea ;
Thy face, pale in the shadowy even,
   Thy quiet eyes that gaze on me !

Oh, realize the moment's charm,
  Thou dearest! We are at life's best,
Folded in God's encircling arm,
  Wave-cradled thus, and wind-caressed!

CELIA THAXTER.

A WET SHEET AND A FLOWING SEA.

A WET sheet and a flowing sea,—
  A wind that follows fast,
That fills the white and rustling sail,
  And bends the gallant mast,—
And bends the gallant mast, my boys,
  While, like the eagle free,
Away the good ship flies, and leaves
  Old England on the lee.

Oh for a soft and gentle wind!
  I heard a fair one cry;
But give to me the snoring breeze,
  And white waves heaving high,—
And white waves heaving high, my boys,
  The good ship tight and free;
The world of waters is our home,
  And merry men are we.

There's tempest in yon hornèd moon,
  And lightning in yon cloud;
And hark the music, mariners!
  The wind is piping loud,—

The wind is piping loud, my boys,
  The lightning flashing free ;
While the hollow oak our palace is,
  Our heritage the sea.

ALLAN CUNNINGHAM.

SONG.

THERE be none of beauty's daughters
    With a magic like thee ;
And like music on the waters
    Is thy sweet voice to me ;
When, as if its sound were causing
The charmed ocean's pausing,
The waves lie still and gleaming,
And the lulled winds seem dreaming,

And the midnight moon is weaving
    Her bright chain o'er the deep,
Whose breast is gently heaving,
    As an infant's asleep ;
So the spirit bows before thee,
To listen and adore thee
With a full but soft emotion,
Like the swell of summer's ocean.

BYRON.

THE FISHING-SONG.

DOWN in the wide, gray river
 The current is sweeping strong :
Over the wide, gray river
 Floats the fisherman's song.

The oar-stroke times the singing,
 The song falls with the oar ;
And an echo in both is ringing
 I thought to hear no more.

Out of a deeper current
 The song brings back to me
A cry from mortal silence
 Of mortal agony.

Life that was spent and vanished,
 Love that had died of wrong,
Hearts that are dead in living,
 Come back in the fisherman's song.

I see the maples leafing
 Just as they leafed before ;
The green grass comes no greener
 Down to the very shore, —

With the rude strain, swelling, sinking,
 In the cadence of days gone by,
As the oar, from the water drinking,
 Ripples the mirrored sky.

Yet the soul hath life diviner;
  Its past returns no more,
But in echoes, that answer the minor
  Of the boat-song from the shore.

And the ways of God are darkness;
  His judgment waiteth long;
He breaks the heart of a woman
  With a fisherman's careless song.

Rose Terry.

"BREAK, BREAK, BREAK."

BREAK, break, break,
  On thy cold gray stones, O sea!
And I would that my tongue could utter
  The thoughts that arise in me.

Oh, well for the fisherman's boy
  That he shouts with his sister at play!
Oh, well for the sailor lad
  That he sings in his boat on the bay!

And the stately ships go on
  To the haven under the hill;
But oh for the touch of a vanished hand,
  And the sound of a voice that is still!

Break, break, break,
  At the foot of thy crags, O sea!
But the tender grace of a day that is dead
  Will never come back to me.

Alfred Tennyson.

ODE TO NEPTUNE,

On Mrs. W——'s Voyage to England.

By Phillis Wheatly, an African slave in Boston, Oct. 10, 1772.

WHILE raging tempests shake the shore,
While Æolus' thunders round us roar,
And sweep impetuous o'er the plain,
Be still, O tyrant of the main ;
Nor let thy brow contracted frowns betray,
While my Susannah skims the watery way.

The Power propitious hears the lay,
The blue-eyed daughters of the sea
With sweeter cadence glide along,
And Thames responsive joins the song.
Pleased with their note, Sol sheds benign his ray,
And double radiance decks the face of day.

To court thee to Britannia's arms,
Serene the clime and mild the sky ;
Her region boasts unnumbered charms ;
Thy welcome smiles in ev'ry eye.
Thy promise, Neptune, keep ; record my prayer,
Nor give my wishes to the empty air.

REMEMBEREST THOU THE DAY?

From Lermontoff.

REMEMBEREST thou the day when we —
　　Late was the hour — were forced to part?
The night-gun boomed athwart the sea;
　　In painful silence beat each heart;
The lonely day found cloudy close;
　　A heavy mist the landscape palled;
And seemed it, when a shot arose,
　　An echo from the ocean called.

Alone I wander by the flood;
　　And when a gun booms in its might,
I think with pain how once we stood
　　Together on that parting night.
And, as the mournful echoes roll,
　　Muffled along the fluid walls,
From out the caverns of my soul
　　Death answeringly calls and calls.

W. R. ALGER.

LA MER.

DES vastes mers tableau philosophique,
   Tu plais au cœur de chagrins agité :
Quand de ton sein, par les vents tourmenté,
Quand des écueils et des grèves antiques
Sortent des bruits, des voix mélancoliques,
L'âme attendrie en ses rêves se perd,
Et, s'égarant de penser en penser
Comme les flots de murmure en murmure,
Elle se mêle à toute la nature :
Avec les vents, dans le fond des déserts,
Elle gémit le long des bois sauvages,
Sur l'Océan vole avec les orages,
Gronde en la foudre et tonne dans les mers.

Mais quand le jour sur les vagues tremblantes
S'en va mourir ; quand, souriant encor,
Le vieux soleil glace de pourpre et d'or
Le vert changeant des mers étincelantes,
Dans des lointains fuyants et veloutés,
En enfonçant ma pensée et ma vue,
J'aime à créer des mondes enchantés,
Baignés des eaux d'une mer inconnue.
L'ardent désir, des obstacles vainqueur,
Trouve, embellit des rives bocagères,
Des lieux de paix, des îles de bonheur,
Où, transporté par les douces chimères,
Je m'abandonne aux songes de mon cœur.

CHATEAUBRIAND.

LES DEUX ÎLES.

IL est deux isles dont un monde
 Sépare les deux Océans,
Et qui de loin dominent l'onde,
Comme des têtes de géants.
On devine, en voyant leurs cimes,
Que Dieu les tira des abîmes
Pour un formidable dessein ;
Leur front de coups de foudre fume,
Sur leurs flancs nus la mer écume,
Des volcans grondent dans leur sein.

Ces Îles, où le flot se broie
Entre des écueils décharnés,
Sont comme des vaisseaux de proie,
D'une ancre éternelle enchaînés.
La main qui de ces noirs rivages
Disposa les sites sauvages,
Et d'effroi les voulut couvrir,
Les fit si terribles peut-être,
Pour que Bonaparte y pût naître,
Et Napoléon y mourir !

" — Là fut son berceau ! — là sa tombe !"
Pour les siècles, c'en est assez.
Ces mots, qu'un monde naisse ou tombe,
Ne seront jamais effacés.
Sur ces Îles, à l'aspect sombre,
Viendront, à l'appel de son ombre,

Tous les peuples de l'avenir ;
Les foudres qui frappent leurs crêtes,
Et leurs écueils, et leurs tempêtes,
Ne sont plus que son souvenir !

Loin de nos rives, ébranlées
Par les orages de son sort,
Sur ces deux îles isolées
Dieu mit sa naissance et sa mort,
Afin qu'il pût venir au monde
Sans qu'une secousse profonde
Annonçât son premier moment,
Et que sur son lit militaire,
Enfin, sans remuer la terre,
Il pût expirer doucement !

Victor Hugo.

UNE NUIT QU'ON ENTENDAIT LA MER SANS LA VOIR.

QUELS sont ces bruits sourds ?
  Ecouter vers l'onde
Cette voix profonde
Qui pleure toujours
Et qui toujours gronde,
Quoiqu'un son plus clair
Parfois l'interrompe. —
Le vent de la mer
Souffle dans sa trompe !

Comme il pleut ce soir !
N'est-ce pas, mon hôte ?
Là-bas, à la côte,
Le ciel est bien noir,
La mer est bien haute !
On dirait l'hiver ;
Parfois on s'y trompe. —
Le vent de la mer
Souffle dans sa trompe.

Oh ! marins perdus !
Au loin, dans cette ombre,
Sur la nef qui sombre,
Que de bras tendus
Vers la terre sombre !
Pas d'ancre de fer
Que le flot ne rompe. —
Le vent de la mer
Souffle dans sa trompe.

Nochers imprudents !
Le vent dans la voile
Déchire la toile
Comme avec les dents !
Là-haut pas d'étoile !
L'un lutte avec l'air,
L'autre est à la pompe. —
Le vent de la mer
Souffle dans sa trompe.

C'est toi, c'est ton feu
Que le nocher rêve,
Quand le flot s'élève,
Chandelier que Dieu
Pose sur la grève !
Phare au rouge éclair
Que la brume estompe —
Le vent de la mer
Souffle dans sa trompe.

Victor Hugo, Juillet, 1836.

LES DEUX VAISSEAUX.

SOUVENT sur les mers où se joue
    La tempête aux ailes de feu,
Je voyais passer sur ma proue
Le haut mât que le vent secoue
Et pour qui la vague est un jeu !

Ses voiles ouvertes et pleines
Aspiraient le souffle des flots,
Et ses vigoureuses antennes
Balancaient sur les vertes plaines
Ses ponts chargés de matelots.

La lame en vain dans la carrière
Battait en grondant ses sabords,
Il la renvoyait en poussière,
Comme un coursier sème en arrière
La blanche écume de son mors !

Longue course à l'heureux navire !
Disais-je : en trois bonds il a fui !
La vaste mer est son empire,
Son horison n'a que sourire,
Et l'univers est devant lui !

Mais d'une humble voile sur l'onde
Si je distinguais la blancheur
Esquif que chaque lame inonde,
Seule demeure qu'ait au monde,
Le foyer flottant du pêcheur :

Lorsque au soir sur la vague brune,
La suivant du cœur et de l'œil,
Je m'attachais à sa fortune,
Et priais les vents et la lune
De la défendre de l'écueil.

Sous une voile dont l'orage
En lambeaux déroulait les plis,
Je voyais le frêle equipage
Disputer son mât qui surnage
Aux coups du vent et du roulis.

Debout le père de famille
Labourait les flots divisés ;
Le fils manœuvrait, et la fille
Recousait avec son aiguille
La voile ou les filets usés.

Des enfants accroupis sur l'âtre
Soufflaient la cendre du matin,
Et déjà la flamme bleuâtre
Egayait le couple folâtre
De l'espoir d'un frugal festin.

Appuyé au mât qui chancelle,
Et que sa main tient embrassé,
La mère les couvait de l'aile,
Et suspendait à sa mamelle
Le plus jeune a son cou bercé.

Ils n'ont, disais-je, dans la vie
Que cette tente et ses trésors ;
Ces trois planches sont leur patrie,
Et cette terre en vain chérie
Le repousse de tous ses bords !

En vain du palais et d'ombrage
Ce golfe immense est couronné.
Ils n'ont pour tenir au rivage
Que l'anneau rongé par l'orage
De quelque môle abandonné !

Ils n'ont pour fortune et pour joie
Que les refrains de leur couplets,
L'ombre que la voile déploie,
La brise que Dieu leur envoie,
Et ce qui tombe des filets.

ALPHONSE DE LAMARTINE.

LE RETOUR DU MARIN.

"PETITS enfants, vos jeunes yeux
    Entre l'eau qui gronde et les cieux
Ont-ils vu blanchir une voile ?
Celle dont j'ai filé la toile,
Si mon rêve dit l'avenir
Avant l'hiver doit revenir."

"Oui, tantôt sur la roche nue,
En regardant l'errante nue,
Nous avons vu là-bas, là-bas,
Rouler une voile sans mâts."

"Enfants des pauvres matelots
Dont les pères sont sur les flots,
Votre voix peut percer l'orage ;
Criez de tout votre courage !
Dans l'éclair aux sombres couleurs
Voit-on flotter nos trois couleurs ?"

"Non : du haut de la roche nue,
Quand l'éclair déchire la nue,
Sur ce pont qui flotte vers nous
On ne voit qu'un homme à genoux."

"C'est lui fidèle et courageux,
Au fond de mon rêve orageux
Cette nuit je l'ai vu paraître ;
Descendez pour le reconnaître !
Moi, j'ai tant pleuré que mes yeux
Ne verront plus *Jame* qu'aux cieux !"

" Ah, la foudre en crevant la nue
L'a jeté sur la roche nue !
S'il n'a pas cessé de souffrir,
Descendons l'aider à mourir ! "

Et les enfants des matelots
Retirerent Jame des flots.
C'était Jame ! et la fiancée
Vint toucher à sa main glacée
Son doux lien, son anneau d'or ;
Car Jame le portait encore !

Qu'ils sont bien sous la roche nue,
A l'abri de l'errante nue,
Oublieux de leurs mauvais jours,
Morts — et mariés pour toujours !

Mme. Desbordes-Valmore.

INDEX OF AUTHORS.

INDEX OF FIRST LINES.